VEGAS BOSS

ALEXIS ABBOTT

PATHFORGERS PUBLISHING

Get an EXCLUSIVE book, **FREE** just as a thank you for signing up for my newsletter! Plus you'll never miss a new release, cover reveal, or promotion!

http://alexisabbott.com/newsletter

I'm like a statue. My hardened face still as stone, while a bead of water trickles down the side of my glass to the polished railing in front of me. My steely gaze pans across the club floor from the second story balcony overlooking everything in the club. I only move my arm every few minutes to bring my drink to my lips, the stage show grabbing my attention.

I don't make a habit of drinking on the job, but tonight is special.

On the stage below, the strippers are putting on one hell of a show. I can smell their perfume from up here as the lights cast a dull pink glow on the black stage, polished so brightly that every flash glimmers, enticing people like moths to a lamp.

The girls are working the crowds for all they're

worth. Hundreds of bills are being tossed onto the stage while the men hoot and holler under the droning beat of the loud music. In a few minutes, the smell of sweat and lust is going to be thick.

My eyes follow one of the dancers as she arches her back and looks at the crowd upside-down while her thighs hug the bar that spins her around. She winks and blows a kiss to someone in the audience, and I see a laughing grin on her face as money starts flying her way. The way her body moves is like liquid silk suspended in the air.

She's gorgeous. Worth every penny the schlubs down below are throwing at her.

Her hair tickles against the stage as her pink lips pucker and pout, her fingers teasing their way along her skin. She's clearly a professional dancer, not like some of the girls just trying some exhibitionism on for size. She knows just how to work the crowd into a frenzy, and I can barely pull my gaze away.

I have to remind myself that she's not what I'm here for.

Not yet, at least.

People glance over at me from time to time, at my six and a half feet in height, muscular frame, and simple but close-fitting tailored clothes. Their eyes see my silhouette, and they look away, cowed. I'm more of a presence than a person.

This would be the easiest hit in the world, if this club didn't belong to my enemies.

The man I'm here for is talking to a group of men in suits at one of the private tables. I've had my eye on him since he walked out of the back offices. He's a wiry older man in his mid-sixties, white hair with flecks of gray still visible at his temples. He has a hawkish nose and a thin, people-pleasing smile. His suit is tailored, but not what I would call classy. He wears a gaudy purple shirt with a dark blue jacket. Somehow, it fits the aesthetic of the club.

It's easy to tell he's one of the co-owners.

And two weeks ago, he tried to murder one of his girls who wouldn't put out for him.

If that weren't despicable enough on its own, it was a stupid move. If he wanted to be responsible, he could have at least hired a professional to take care of his needs and avoid all this mess. Instead, he decided to try fooling around with a girl barely a third of his age.

The girl escaped. That's an impressive feat. This is one of the oldest Italian clubs in Vegas, and one of the last holdouts of their power here in the city. As it happened, she had connections. Rich connections.

And those connections didn't take kindly to the way she was treated.

When me and the other Russians running business in the city got word of the hit someone put out on the club owner, I thought Christmas had come early.

It's the perfect cover for a takeover.

I lean forward on the railing of the balcony after I finished my drink. The taste of vodka and tonic on my lips keeps the other mixed smells of alcohol in the club away from me. My target has just finished shaking hands and saying a few empty words to the important-looking guests at the table, and he starts making his way to one of the back rooms where his office is.

His name is Dio Morelli, and his life is worth a hell of a lot of money that I plan on cashing in tonight.

"And what about this fucker?"

The sound of a young man's slurred voice behind me makes me quirk an eyebrow. I have a mental picture of him without even turning around. College-age, deep enough voice that he must have a wide, strong frame, and enough alcohol in him to knock a lesser man out cold.

"Hey, I'm talkin' to you!" he shouts at me, but I don't even flinch. "You checkin' out my girl, asshole?"

"Curt, he can't hear you," a second voice grunts. The club music is throbbing in my ears, but I can hear their voices perfectly clearly.

"Let's check his hearing," the man called Curt slurs, and heavy footsteps tell me he's coming up beside me. The next second, he appears at my side, catching himself before leaning too far over the side of the balcony. "Hey, jackass? Quit staring at my girl down there!"

Slowly, I turn my head barely an inch toward him and raise an eyebrow.

"Your girl?" I say simply.

"Yeah," he barks, and he points down to the stripper center-stage down below, who's now doing splits on the bar and has enough cash on the stage to buy a round for all the other girls, if she wanted. "I got a VIP pass, and I'm gonna make her mine later tonight, so piss off to some other club!"

I'm vaguely amused.

"Curt, forget this asshole," the man's friend calls.

"Listen to your friend," I warn him in a casual tone.

I know that's just going to piss him off, though, and the vein that throbs in his forehead tells me I'm right. Normally, I wouldn't even bother with small potatoes like him. But he's made the bad move of getting my attention.

His hand flashes forward, intending to knock the drink out of my hand.

The moment his hand moves, I swiftly yet calmly set the drink on the railing a foot away from me, just barely evading his swipe, and with my other hand, I simply take his wrist.

I don't even increase my heart rate as I twist his arm around his back and whip his whole frame around. I do so just in time to put him between me and his friend, who was throwing a punch at the back of my head. Instead, the blow catches Curt in the jaw, and I hear a tooth clatter to the ground with the flecks of blood that go flying.

I squeeze Curt's wrist until I hear a painful pop, and I thrust him forward into his friend. I was right —the two men are about the size and build of football players, and they're both glassy-eyed enough that I know they're closer to getting thrown out than being let into the VIP room.

Once the two men collide, Curt starts throwing punches wildly, thinking I'm the one in front of him. The moment his first punch connects with his friend, I reach around his waist and slip two fingers into his pocket. Curt's VIP ticket is poking out. I grab it, pocket it, take my drink, and calmly walk away as the two friends start throwing blows at each other.

By the time I'm setting my glass on the bar and giving the bartender a nod, security is already busy trying to get the men to break up. It's a task easier said than done, considering both the men are pushing three-hundred pounds.

I make my way down the stairs and check the time on my phone. Twelve-thirty in the morning. I've lost sight of my target, but I have his schedule memorized. He's a creature of habit, and I know exactly where he is, unless something's gone awry.

And I spend enough time planning every hit that I do *not* make mistakes.

Right about now, every night, he goes out back for a smoke with two of the meanest bastards on the security crew with him as bodyguards. That would be easy enough, if he didn't also take the other club owner with him on his breaks.

Personally, I'd love to deal with both of them in one quick and clean bloodbath. There's a pistol strapped to my leg and a silencer in my jacket. Four quick shots, and they'd all be down.

Usually, the next course of action would be to simply follow the target home and deal with him there.

But tonight is special.

Tonight, I'm sending a message.

The exit my target will have used is through the dancer's rooms and offices, meaning I can't get to them from the inside. I'll have to take an outside approach.

I slip out of the club and wade through the crowds of people in the streets of Vegas until I can slip into one of the steamy alleyways behind the club. A rat scurries out of my way as I make my way down the shadowy street, my footsteps silent.

The alley is wide enough for a car to pass through, and there's nothing blocking the path. This is the way the owners pulled up in their expensive sports cars. I stick to the shadows and stay low as I near the edge of the building.

Voices reach my ears as I get there, and I glance just far enough around the corner to see the four figures standing there.

One of the guards is standing with the two owners. The other is standing at the door, his arms crossed. As I suspected, there are a few cars parked in the little lot back here, and there's only one steady light illuminating the place.

That's all the cover I need.

Silent as a shadow, I get low and wait for a time when none of their eyes are looking my way before I dart out and start sliding through the cars to get closer to the men.

Their voices reach me as I get close enough that it's time to take my pistol out and screw on the silencer.

"Dunno why you can't just use the fuckin' lounge we paid out the ass for to have your smokes, Dio," his partner is saying with a dark chuckle. "I think you just like making us feel like the girls, having to come out here."

"Easier for James here to go get us a coffee without getting distracted by the girls up to the lounge," Dio shoots back with a slap on his guard's shoulder. The guard cracks a stony smile at him. "Besides, it's a nice lounge, let's just keep the fuckin' smoke out of it for another month or two before we start ruining it."

"Yeah, yeah," his partner laughs. A moment later, his tone gets more serious. "So, that business last week. With the girl."

"Christ, Frank, this again?" Dio groans. "I've got it handled."

"I'm just trying to make sure we don't get blindsided by anything," Frank says. "With the Russians trying to bust down the gates, I don't need any more surprises. She might have been a little cunt, but she had some connections out west."

"We won't have to worry about blowback from the Russians on this one," Dio says, and I'm mildly surprised. "Report from Carlo says they've got some internal trouble. Change in leadership might be on the table very soon. Some top-level old guard schmucks on the chopping block. They won't be looking outward to make money off vendettas anytime soon."

My eyebrows go up, and my fist tightens around my pistol.

This is news to me, and I *don't* like getting news like that from my enemies.

I want to wait and listen for more. If this is the first tip I'm getting about something big happening in my mafia, that's not a good sign for my position. Something's afoot.

But every second I spend waiting is another second I risk losing this job.

"Alright, big guy, get us a couple of coffees from the place around the corner, will you?"

I take out a ski mask from my jacket and slip it over my head.

As soon as I hear the guard step down from the ramp leading up to the back door, my Spetsnaz training kicks into action.

I pop up over the hood of the car I'm hiding behind with my pistol out. In a fraction of an instant, the four men freeze. In that fraction of a second, I take aim and pull the trigger.

There's a soft *thunk* as a hole appears in Dio Morelli's right eye, and his body falls to its knees before folding to the ground, cigarette falling off the ramp.

That was the easy part.

I vault over the hood of the car and sprint toward the other three men. The guards are reaching for their guns, and Frank is staggering toward the door. I have about six seconds.

In the first two seconds, I clear the distance between me and the first guard who was about to get coffee. Before he can even look up from drawing his gun, mine is out, and I pistol-whip him squarely on the forehead without breaking my pace. His heavy body hits the ground, unconscious.

In the next two seconds, I leap up the ramp and

dive, not for Frank, but for the second guard in front of the door. Our bodies collide, but my hand clenches his face as I crash against the door with him padding the impact. As hard as I can, I slam the back of his head into the metal door. I release him and watch him sway a moment, dazed, and another quick punch to his nose drops him. His heavy frame blocks the doorway.

In the last two seconds, I turn to see Frank sprinting away from me, toward his car. I take off after him, and it's like a hawk chasing down a rabbit.

I catch him from behind and wrap my arms behind his head.

"Jesus fuck!" he whimpers as soon as he realizes I've got him. "L-look, I don't know who the fuck sent you, but I'll double their price! What do you want? One of the girls? I've got more blow in the back than any other club in Vegas, you want that?"

I say nothing to him. If he so much as hears my voice, it could endanger my mission.

Instead, I turn him around and start walking him slowly back to his partner's body.

"You cock-sucker," he rasps when he sees Dio's dead body. I tighten the grip on him until I feel one of his shoulders pop, and he lets out a grunt of pain. "If you're gonna do this, make it quick."

I walk him right up to the body, then shift my grip on him to put him in a sleeper hold. He starts to struggle, but I keep a tight grip on him until I feel his body go limp in my arms as he passes out. I hold up his dead weight and make sure he's unconscious before I take my pistol and put it in his hand. I guide his hand to aim the gun at Dio's head, and I pull the trigger. Another *thunk*, and I've just incriminated Frank for the murder of his partner.

I unscrew the silencer, wipe the gun down, and leave it wrapped in Frank's hand. There's a good chance the guards' memories will be fuzzy when they wake up. Regardless, I'd like there to be a little confusion about what exactly happened out here and hedge the risk that they'll dare let an investigation take place over Dio's murder.

Evidence planted, I slip away, silently as I came.

I'm a second generation Russian here in Vegas. We've been slowly pushing our way into the scene, chipping away at the Italians since the cops cracked down on the city and made it too family-friendly for the old Italians to keep up. We run aggressive businesses, but they're legitimate.

Soon, this will be one of several newly taken over Russian clubs. And I have no doubt that the staff will welcome the new management.

In the meantime, I pull the VIP pass out of my pocket and look it over.

I'd like to enjoy a little time to myself in this club before the bodies get found.

After a little thought, though, I tear the pass in two and toss it into a garbage can before I exit the alley and start walking back to my car half an hour away.

I didn't make it to the top by wasting time, blowing off steam, as much as I might have to blow off.

I got here by being the best.

I'd like to see my rivals *try* to shake me.

I can feel the music pulsing like a heartbeat under my toes, the bass bumping and vibrating the glossy wooden stage underneath me. It's a song I used to listen to as a teenager, dancing and singing into my hairbrush in the relative privacy of my bedroom. I would lip sync in front of the mirror, tossing my hair around, pretending to be whatever singer or pop star I was into at the time. It was a welcome break from the hours and hours of studying I put in, since I was determined to make perfect grades and get more scholarships than anyone else in my class.

I have always been that way: a diehard perfectionist. When I commit to something, I don't do it halfway. I throw my entire mind, body, and soul into it. Which is why, right now, I am determined to dance and groove better than any other girl out here.

This stage is just another competitive playing field on which I will show the world what I'm made of. I have to wear the highest stilettos. I have to have the most shimmery skin. I have to wear the laciest, sexiest ensemble this crowd has ever seen.

I have to seduce everyone who walks in through those doors. And at the end of the night, I will have more dollars tucked into the elastic band of my thong than anyone else.

Especially if the DJ keeps playing songs like this one. I glance over at the disk jockey booth, where the man, whose name I think is Anton, is hanging out watching all the dancers. He's a skinny young guy with a mop of curly brown hair and a lip ring, and sometimes he's so distracted by the seductive routines the girls put on to pay attention to his job.

He's not there to gawk. It's not supposed to be a free show. He's there to play hot music that is easy for us to dance to, but Anton can't be much older than eighteen, and this is a teenage boy's paradise.

I manage to catch his eye as he stares at me, open-mouthed, a glazed look over his face. Not interrupting my dance routine for a second, I subtly raise an eyebrow at him and give a little nod, to remind him that he has a job to do. His face flushes pink with embarrassment when he realizes he's been caught drooling over the talent again, and he quickly whips around to look down at his turntable again.

I don't even pretend to stifle my smile of amusement. I simply turn to look back at the small crowd gathering around my stage. There's not a single woman to be seen in the clientele space. The only women here are the ones hard at work, each hustling and shimmying to entice a well-paying customer to her stage, to seduce crotchety old men and bored, sleazy business execs out of their cash.

It's not an easy job, and my time here has been more than enough to convince me that these women are tough, capable, and smart. And now that I'm one of them, it's my goal to become the toughest, the most capable, and the smartest of all. Because every single guy who passes through the entrance might just be the jackpot I'm looking for.

I do a slow, sensual twirl with my arms stretched up over my head, biting my lip as I tilt my head back and shake my hair out. I know my hair is one of my most striking attributes, shiny auburn waves that cascade to about the middle of my back.

One time, years ago, a sweet older woman told me it looked like a freshly-fallen autumn leaf, with its tones of brown and reddish gold. My little sister calls it "cinnamon." Either way, I know enough about this line of work to emphasize every little gift genetics has given me.

I sway from side to side, rocking my hips in a smooth, fluid motion while I run my fingers back through my hair. I close my eyes for a second and let out a soft, sexy moan. I know all these men watching me are imagining what I would sound like in bed. They are all picturing me naked, arching my back and crying out in pleasure. It's exactly what I want them to think about while they watch me dance.

That old adage is true: sex sells. And here, at this dimly-lit strip club hanging off the tail end of the strip in Las Vegas, sex sells like hotcakes. These men with deep pockets and time to kill come strolling through the door to shop around for an experience they can deposit in the spank bank or brag about to their equally sleazy buddies around the water cooler.

It's a fantasy I'm putting up for sale, a dream I can toss into the crowd as easily as blowing a kiss. I can make them wish I belonged to them. And if they are willing to pay, I can even give them just enough hope to imagine that might be possible.

Of course, it isn't. I'm not here to shop for a boyfriend.

Sure, I might be one sexy, sparkly piece of bait dangling from a fishing line so I can reel in wealthy perverts and clean out their pockets, but they don't get to take their prize home. This club, this stage, this routine, is my fish bowl, and nobody is going to scoop me out. When these horny guys go home, they go home alone. Or at least, if not alone, they're not leaving with me.

It's important to make them think there's a chance, but it's even more important to stay safe and professional.

I open my eyes again as I rotate slowly, bringing my arms down so I can caress my neck, my shoulders, my breasts. I never used to be the kind of woman who spent money on frivolous treats like manicures, but nowadays, it's become vital. I have to make certain that every single inch of my body plays into the fantasy of the perfect woman. I have to embody perfection itself, and if that means shelling out cash for flawlessly round, smooth French tips, then so be it.

What is it they say?

You have to spend money to make money.

I cup my ample breasts in my palms, licking my lips as I bend down in my stilettos. I give the crowd a salacious grin and a wink, making sure they pay attention when I slide my hands down my chest, over my taut, hard stomach.

I have always been the type to stay in shape, but these days it's even more important to keep everything tight. Of course, it helps that dancing itself is a great workout. I run my hands down my abdominal muscles to my pelvis, teasing my onlookers, making them think I might touch myself. But instead I just slide my hands along the insides of my thighs toward my knees, shaking my ass while I'm bent over.

I'm still wearing a tight bodycon dress in a velvety dark red hue, the color of blood or roses. It's a few sizes too small, which means that it's a perfect fit here in the context of the strip club. It barely grazes the tops of my thighs, exposing glimpses of my black thong underneath, which is exactly what I want. And it's so tight up top that my black, lacy push-up bra is visible, peeking through. My cleavage is on prominent display.

Some of the other dancers wear more, others wear considerably less even at the start of their routines. But I like to start out with just enough skin showing to tease my clientele without giving it all away or looking too buttoned-up. My stilettos are black, with tight laces crisscrossing up my ankles and calves. When I first bought them a few days ago, I worried that I might look like a sexy gladiator or something with these strappy heels, but so far, so good. Maybe these guys are into the sexy gladiator look.

Or maybe, more likely, my breasts are just far more interesting to look at than my choice in shoes.

I know I look pretty damn good, and it's clear that my customers agree. The newer customers are looking around, shopping for the girl they want to patronize most tonight. I have learned from my observations that most of them tend to select one dancer to follow around and haunt for the night, rather than moving from one stage to another.

A lot of the older, more experienced customers tend to stick with the same girl every time. They learn her schedule and show up specifically for her shifts. They build up a relationship, however one-sided, and maintain it like a prized garden, visiting often to water the seeds and watch the fantasy grow fuller and stronger.

It doesn't really matter that it's all for show. They are more discerning than I would have expected, which is good news for me. It just means I have to work extra hard to be the most interesting, the most tantalizing, the most irresistible. I need those return customers, but I need to reel in the newcomers, too.

After all, any one of them could be the man I'm hunting for.

One of my favorite moves is to make intense, unbreakable eye contact. I have found that to be one of the best ways to ensure a client stays put. It makes him feel wanted. Involved. Like he's as much a part of the dance as I am, even though all he has to do is sit down and get comfortable and keep feeding dollars my way. In front of me right now there are three men lounging against the black faux-leather sofas while the neon lights dance across their faces.

There's one older, possibly middle-aged, guy in a sleazy suit, the top three buttons undone and his tie loosened, hanging askew over his shoulder. His graying hair is all tousled, which makes me think he has probably already gotten a lap dance or two. He has that smarmy, smug expression on his face.

He might be difficult to reel in, since he's already been in the VIP room with at least one other dancer.

I might just be his cooldown, and he doesn't look wealthy or connected enough to be my target. I quickly discard him as a main focus.

The second guy looks barely old enough to be here, his face red and his eyes wide and round as saucers. He's holding a weak well drink, probably made with some barely-drinkable whiskey and off-brand soda. He's wearing jeans and a tucked-in white polo, which is a bad choice, because it shows up just how skinny and sweaty he is. He's nervous. This is probably his first time, and he's still half-worried that his mom might bust in here at any moment and drag him home by the ear.

I give him a wink and bite my lip, not because he looks like the type I'm looking for, but because it gives me a thrill of amusement to watch this scrawny young man blush and get flustered when I give him some attention. He nearly chokes on his crappy mixed drink, his mouth hanging open as though he's shocked that I even noticed him. I have to quickly turn and face the other way, shaking my ass so that I get a chance to giggle without him noticing.

And the third man isn't exactly on the sofa. He's standing a few feet away from the others, cast almost entirely in shadow. He's got his arms folded over his chest, and I can just barely make out the bulkiness of his silhouette. This guy is ripped, muscular all over, with a serious, almost contemplative look on his face.

He is exceedingly handsome, but I know I should be annoyed that he's standing back and watching me from afar. If he's really interested, he should come closer and give me money. I don't dance to be judged, I dance to get paid.

But something about him just lights a fire deep inside of me. It's like he's a match, scratching against the friction of my body rolling and swaying in my tight outfit, making me feel hot and, admittedly, a little turned on. There's just something different about the way he's watching me, something unnamable that sets him apart from the other guys staring at me longingly.

They all look at me, knowing how unattainable I am. But this mystery man looks at me like an equal. Like we're just two people meeting by chance, by destiny.

Has fate brought him here to me today? Is he the one I've been looking for?

The older man stands up and slides me a hundred-dollar bill. That's the cue. I manage to rip my eyes away from the mystery man long enough to step down off the stage and stand in front of my older patron. I reach out and set my hands on his shoulders, swaying and undulating my hips while he watches me intently. Someone is on a roll today. I wonder how many other dancers he's paid for tonight already. Not that it matters. Money is money.

I begin to dance for him, forcing myself to focus just on the older man. Catching the cue, the young guy moves off to another stage, giving us privacy.

But that mystery guy in the shadows doesn't move a muscle. In fact, when I glance over at him, my heart skips a beat.

He is still staring.

That intense stare blazing right through to my soul. I should be pissed off that this guy is getting a free show, but instead, it just turns me on to know he's watching me.

My fingers graze up along my collarbone as I flip my hair, my heart thudding louder in my chest as I roll my hips. I'm not a raunchy dancer. I try to use my sensuality, more than anything, and I can hear my client's breath catch as I tilt my cleavage towards him.

But my gaze is over his head, to the side.

I bite my lip seductively as it dawns on me that I'm not even dancing for the attention of my actual paying customer. I'm really dancing for the mystery guy.

My fingers roam down between my breasts, teasing my skin as I feel true desire and excitement swell between my thighs. I've never felt so excited in all my time here, and knowing I've so captivated such a delicious looking man is like an aphrodisiac.

My fantasies run amok as I turn, arching my back and letting them both look at my ass, watch my hand as it teases the bodycon up over my skin, tantalizingly revealing myself.

Luckily, my patron is utterly oblivious to the way I move my body for someone just off to the side. Throughout my whole routine, the mystery man doesn't look away for even a second, until right before I'm finished, when he walks off.

I take another hundred-dollar bill from my client with thanks, only a little embarrassed by how distracted I was.

But someone else has gotten under my skin. I'm intrigued now. He's got *me* hooked.

I skip my break altogether, too focused on finding him to rest. The crowd is thick this time of night and it takes me a while to wade through the half-naked dancers and the drunken, eager hands of the clients. I have to turn down several requests for dances before I finally spot him sitting in a dark corner of the lounge with a booth all to himself.

Jackpot.

I saunter up to him, trying my best to look both interested and detached. It's a delicate balance.

When he sees me, he gives me a slow, knowing smile. He calls me over with a nod of his head. He's even better looking up close: heavily muscled, tall, rugged features. Jet-black hair and piercing blue eyes. There's something vaguely wolfish about him, something almost predatory. I know that he could snap me in half without breaking a sweat, and while that should probably frighten me, it just turns me on even more.

He's got to be the one.

"I saw you watching me," I purr, tucking my hair behind my ears. "If you want a private dance, all you have to do is pay up."

"I know how it works, *malyshka*," he growls in response, raising a heavy, dark eyebrow. "But I like to know what I'm paying for before I buy it."

I'm speechless. I know I should be angry or offended. If it were anyone else, I would be. Instead, my feelings are... complicated.

"So, dance for me," he commands in a low, gruff voice. He curls his finger, silently demanding for me to come closer. He sets a few hundred-dollar bills on the table. My heart begins to race.

The faint accent.

The Russian term of endearment.

The stack of money on the table.

This has to be my guy.

I sway and spin slowly, running my hands up and down my body, giving it my all. This is the dance of my life, and I have to do it right. I watch his eyes, never breaking my gaze even as I look back at him over my shoulder, grinding my ass into his lap, sliding my fingertips along his powerful thighs through his tailored slacks.

I turn back around and straddle him, rolling my hips while I caress his chiseled jaw, the faint prickly stubble there. I can smell my perfume, the hint of sweetness, mingling with his cologne and the scent of his body into a heady cocktail that makes my heart flutter.

This time, it's all I can do to keep from picturing him naked.

I run my hands down his strong arms and can't help but wonder how it must feel to have him pick me up and throw me around. Those bright blue eyes never tear away from me, and hardly a flicker crosses his face while I tease and seduce him. He's like a marble statue, unmovable except for the bright fire burning in his gaze. I let the dance drag on much longer than I normally would, not wanting to leave him for even a second.

As far as I'm concerned, he's the one.

Now I just have to find my way in.

I lean in close, my arms lightly around his neck, breathing softly against the side of his face. He turns and whispers roughly, "I'm sold. I'm taking you home."

"Straight to the point, huh?" I reply flirtatiously, even as my stomach twists into knots.

He's giving me a way in, but I don't know if I should take it. This isn't the way it's supposed to be done. This is not protocol. I may be in pretty deep, but I know well enough to be careful about blurring the lines between ruse and reality.

On the one hand, it's taken a lot of pulling strings and calling in favors to get here, and now that I'm this close to the jackpot, how can I possibly pull out?

On the other hand… well, going home with a suspected mafia boss is not exactly the most appropriate action for an undercover cop to take.

But if I want to infiltrate his organization and learn all its secrets, all its transgressions, then I have to get closer. I have to keep up this image as long as I can, whatever it takes.

Weeks of training, planning, and preparation have gone into this mission, and I'm honored to be the one in the spotlight. It's risky as hell, but I didn't become a police officer just to sit behind a desk and file paperwork all day. This is what I have to do to make a name for myself, to live up to my father's legacy, to make my department proud.

"I'm a man who knows what he wants. And tonight, I want you," my target replies, his breath ticklish on my neck. How the hell am I supposed to say no? My body is on fire, every nerve burning with desire for this sexy, dangerous man.

I try to reason with myself, find a way to justify the leap of faith and breach of protocol I'm about to take. The closer I get to my subject, the closer I get to the truth, to the crime, to the arrest. The glory.

The satisfaction of a job well done and a crime solved.

And what better way to get close than to sleep with the enemy?

After all, I am nothing if not dedicated to my job.

"Take me home," I whisper back, "and I'll show you what else this body can do."

In the elevator, we can't keep our hands off each other. Her fingers are daring, exploring every inch of my body she can get to. Every time she finds some new ripple in my statuesque form, she seems to get more excited, more turned on, more desperate.

I have to admit, it's refreshing.

I never let myself cut loose and enjoy the night, but this girl has awakened something in me I didn't think I'd ever spare the time to feel. Everything about her makes me crave something sinful, and tonight, I'm going to give her all that and then some.

Our lips are inseparable. I have her pinned to the wall of the elevator, my hands on her hips, sliding around to her ass, pulling her just a little closer to grind her against my crotch. She can feel how hard I am for her, and I feel the heat between her legs.

She puts her arms up on my shoulders as I lift her up to kiss her more comfortably, and she giggles into my mouth. I finally break away with a wet smack and move to her neck, teasing the flesh with my teeth.

I hear her soft sigh in my ear, and it makes my cock throb with need.

"This elevator takes forever," she whispers. "I like it."

I grope her breast, and she bites her lip.

"It's a long way to the top floor."

Her eyes widen and shimmer as she realizes I own the penthouse suite. It's such an irresistible face that I can't help but attack her again, taking that full lower lip of hers between my teeth and teasing them before she pulls me into a full kiss.

I flick the switch on when we arrive at my destination and fill the penthouse with soft white light. Her eyes widen as she gasps. It's a soft noise against my chest that makes my heart thud harder. Once the place is lit up, she steps inside slowly, looking around in awe and wonder like a deer seeing snow in the forest for the first time.

My apartment is more like a hotel suite than an actual home. I'm rarely here, so I keep the place very clean for unexpected company like this. It's a modern interior, with sleek gray floors, black walls, and sparse plants here and there to keep the place fresh.

And, of course, the far wall of the penthouse is just one great stretch of full-panel windows overlooking the Las Vegas Strip, letting the dull glow of neon signs from the city that never sleeps right into my living room. I can dim them whenever I want by turning on a tinting effect in the windows.

I was about to do just that before I see the girl walking toward the window in wonder, her mouth hanging open.

When she looks back at me with a genuinely excited smile on her face, I feel my heart melt. I wonder if the club who hired this girl knows just how much of a delight she is.

It's not likely. If they realized she was going home with clients, she'd probably be fired. It's a liability, mixing strippers and escorts in a strip club.

"I've been in some nice apartments before, at the parties the other girls throw, but I've never had a view like this," she gushes.

"You like it?" I ask, slipping my jacket off and tossing it onto the red leather couch as I approach her from behind. Near the window, I put my hands on her hips and loom over her, letting her lean back into me.

"We don't have anything like this in my hometown. It doesn't get old, does it?"

"No," I lie.

I wonder if she really thinks I live here. The place looks about as unlived-in as it could get. This woman has me intrigued, and she must know that. I want to keep digging past the layers of the act and see what I can really tease out of her.

"What's your name, girl? Or would you like me to just keep calling you that all night?"

She bites her lip and giggles, turning her head so the neon lights below us catch in her beautiful hazel eyes, green and brown layered and mingling with each other. "I wouldn't mind that... but my name's Misty."

I'm good at catching liars. You don't get to where I am in the *bratva* by having a trusting heart, but you don't have to be a genius to know that she's giving a stage name. I give her a knowing smile, but I squeeze her hips and pull her close into my still-hard cock.

"Very well, Misty," I grant her, which she seems to appreciate. She wiggles closer into my chest and lets out a soft sigh. "I'm Misha."

"Misha?" she asks, tilting her head to the side. "Where's that from?"

"Russia," I say, letting a little accent slip through that makes her smile.

"I never would have guessed."

"My family has been here a long time," I whisper in a husky tone in her ear, and I slip my hands around to her front, sliding down toward the waist of her skirt. "This city has been my home for all my life. In my own ways, I run this place."

"Really?" she asks, barely above a whisper.

"Let me show you how," I reply, and I slip my fingers into her panties.

My warm touch brushes against her slit, and she draws in a sharp breath. She's already wet and hot down there, and she digs her fingers into my pant leg. Regardless of how much of her personality is an act, that's one thing that she can't lie about.

"Do you want this?" I ask as I start to swirl my fingers around her swollen nub, touching the wet clit and teasing it just enough to make her push her hips into it, almost on reflex. "Do you want me inside you, Misty?"

"I want it," she whimpers, and my other hand goes up under her top. I peel off the nipple covers and toss them to the floor so I can feel her stiff buds with my own fingertips. There's just that little hint of shame to her tone. She doesn't want to want this as bad as she does.

I like that.

"Tell me what you want," I say. "Beg for it."

"I want you to fuck me, Misha," she says without hesitation, pushing her ass into my crotch and making me ache with need. "Fuck me against the window. Don't hold anything back."

"If there's one thing you're going to learn about me, Misty," I growl into her ear before I hitch her skirt up to her waist and pull her panties down to her knees, making her gasp, "it's that I *never* hold back."

I unbutton my pants and grab my pulsing cock, pinning it between us. She feels it against her ass, and she gasps, pushing against it needfully. I grind against her and pin her to the window with her back to me, savoring the feeling of her soft flesh surrounding my dick for a few moments.

"Holy shit," she gasps as she feels just how thick and hard I am for her.

"Second thoughts?" I growl as I take hold of her hips, fingers digging into curvy flesh.

"God, no," she whimpers, and I feel fire flaring up in my body. I know liars. I've been around them my whole life, and I can tell when a woman is just after money or power.

She's after my body. I'm going to enjoy this girl more than I thought.

I lift her up easily in my strong hands and let my cock stick straight up between her legs. She presses her hands and knees to the window, breathing fast, but she's not flailing helplessly. She's a stripper. She's in good shape, and she can handle this with no problem.

I push my hips up to give her pussy a feel of the dark, swollen crown that's desperate to get into her. As soon as it touches, I groan. My cock throbs at how hot and wet she is.

"Do you want a condom?" I whisper.

"I'm on the pill," she whimpers back. "Please, Misha, don't keep me waiting!"

The words are barely out of her mouth before I impale her on my cock.

She gives a squeal of delight that cracks adorably in her throat. I'm only halfway in her, not wanting to hurt her, but the tip of my cock has gone straight in to strike her g-spot, that sensitive place that's been aching to get stroked all evening.

I start working my cock back and forth through her tight, wet flesh. Immediately, I feel her start to tear through they layers and layers of tension I've had wound up in my body.

With her hands and knees pressed against the window, her feet are against my thighs, and her back is arched backward to accommodate my monstrously thick shaft. She's an incredible acrobat, otherwise this would hardly be possible.

And it's more worth it than I could have imagined.

I thought I'd had all the pleasures that Vegas had to offer, but pinning "Misty" to the window on my cock is proving to be the best yet, and it's only getting started.

I start thrusting back and forth, holding her hips in a strong grip. I have utter control over the situation. Any way she wants to turn, she has to beg my hands with her body, and I'll consider her request before granting it or turning her a way I prefer.

My cock gets two-thirds of the way in, and her sighing is starting to sound like a desperate panting.

Her slickness is all over my cock, and I start getting more regular, more precise. Each time I buck up into her, I feel her ass press against me, and I want to slap it pink and make her cry my name.

That will come, though.

I start to get faster and faster until I know her insides so intimately I can go directly where I want to without a second thought. As if on a track, my cock slides all the way out, leaving just that bulging crown in to tease the outside of her pussy, then so far in that my tip and the soft underside of my cock gets ground against her g-spot, and with every few thrusts, I feel her pussy pulse and tighten around me.

Her heat is so intense that there may as well be hot coals between us, driving into each other with every thrust. My abs are like a finely tuned machine that works in perfect harmony with the rest of my body to give her all the pleasure someone like her deserves.

She can feel the way my powerful forearms turn her this way and that when I want a new angle on her, exploring new parts of her that I only can with a body like mine. My legs are like iron. I could keep her up here for hours and not do so much as twitch from the strain.

Still, it's a workout for both of us. The scent of our sweat mixes with my cologne and her perfume as I fuck her faster and harder, so used to the feeling of her g-spot that it's like second nature to me.

Her pussy is fertile ground that I will plough until it gives me what I want.

And by the time there are handprints on the cold window, her whole body starts to tense up, and I know I'm about to get that blossom I've been working for.

In a risky move, I take one hand off her hips and take hold of her hair, pulling it back just enough that she knows I'm holding her tight.

"Say my name, girl," I growl. I angle my hips so they can help support her while I bounce her on my cock to keep the pace up. I'm like a piston hammering up into her, and the blush I see on her neck tells me how much she's feeling it. "I want to hear it on those lips of yours."

She can only pant and groan in response, so I turn the pressure up. I start bucking harder and faster, letting myself go just enough so that my cock pulses and throbs with pleasure up into her. I'm on the brink of releasing into her, but I'm not letting go just yet. I let a bead of precum well up inside her and mix with her honey.

My grip on her hair and her hips gets tighter the more I fuck her, and it feels like her body is a bow I'm pulling back, about to let fly.

Then, all at once, her whole body convulses, and she gives a ragged scream. "Oh god, Misha!"

The cry comes with the sweetest sigh I've ever heard in my life. I'm so close to coming that the slightest loss of control could send me over the edge, but I am a master of self-control.

Instead of coming in her, I slow down as I feel her wet my cock with the course of her orgasm. Her limbs are shaking, but I'm only giving her a short break.

I slide her off my cock delicately and carry her in my arms as she goes limp.

"Did... did you finish?" she asks wearily through panting breaths while I carry her back to my room. I smile wickedly down at her.

"If you think we're finished, you're in for a ride, little Misty," I growl.

Once we reach the bed, I toss her on it, watching her bounce uselessly. "Strip," I order her, and she regains her composure enough to obey my command. She gets up on her shaky knees to start taking her top off in a slow, seductive tease that makes my lip curl up.

My bed is massive, but its black sheets serve as the perfect stage for her to reveal herself on. I pace around it, stalking like a hungry wolf as I watch her lose her top, looking over her shoulder at me with smoky, lustful eyes that promise so much. I reward her efforts by taking my own shirt off, revealing the wall of muscles underneath.

She bites her lip at the sight. She wants to touch me dearly, but I'm not coming closer yet. She knows what she has to do. I nod to her skirt, and she bobs her head obediently before teasing the fabric off her legs, along with her panties. Once it's all spread out on the bed, she lays back and splays herself out, ready for me. The way her limbs writhe in the sheets makes me want to attack her right then and there.

And I'm about to.

I kick my shoes off and strip off the rest of my clothes. My cock is stiff and bobbing, still glistening with her honey, and my heavy balls are swinging under my shaft with each step toward her.

When I'm finally close enough, I swing a leg over her, positioning me over her body. I lower myself so that our faces are only inches apart, and I feel her hands exploring my warm flesh.

"How are you this hard?" she half-jokes, her blushing face growing a shade redder.

"I like to impress," I joke right back with a boyish grin.

She worries her lip as she starts to run her nails down my hardened pecs, but her eyes go wide when I prod her pussy with my tip, reminding her just what's still to come.

"Are you ready for more?" I growl.

"No," she confesses, "but I need it, *now*."

I like 'Misty'.

My hands go to her breasts, and I squeeze them, feeling their soft firmness and the hardened nubs at the center of them. As I do, I slide my cock into her, and she gasps so sharply that you'd think I'd entered her for the first time.

Immediately, my cock remembers where it is, and even from this new angle, it's like I've known it for years. I sit up and wrap her legs around my hips before I start bucking into her, picking up right where I left off.

My thumbs massage and toy with her nipples while the V of my lower abs thrusts back and forth. Her hazel eyes are watching it hungrily, devouring my whole body. I want her to leave here with the memory of a man she'll never forget.

The next time she touches herself, I'm going to be on her mind, like she'll be on mine.

My swollen balls hit her ass with each thrust as I start to get harder and faster. I go deeper than I ever have before, nearly my entire spear lodged deep inside her at the apex of every buck.

Resting on the bed, my body can go even harder and faster than before. I piston into her with more and more precision. The tip of my cock, already spilling precum into her depths, hits the same spot over and over again, and I feel her body winding up again for me, her mouth falling open to show her shining white teeth past gorgeous, full lips.

"I'm going to make you come, Misty," I promise her, "and when I'm done with you, you'll need to take a night off work."

"As long as I can spend it with you," she whimpers, a warm smile on her face as I drive her closer and closer to the edge. It's so rare that I meet a woman who really knows what she wants, who's so in tune with her body that she can confidently stride into sex with someone like me and get every bit of enjoyment I want to give her.

She tries to grip the sheets, and I take my hands from her breasts to pin her wrists up over her head, paralyzing her, making her more vulnerable to me as I go harder and harder.

Finally, she arches her back like it was a few minutes ago, and I feel her whole body let loose yet again, the sweet orgasm shaking her whole body. She writhes under me, and this time, I don't let up.

I keep pounding into her at the same rhythm. Her body tries to squirm away from me, but I don't let it. Her reflexes are useless. I'm stimulating her to the point that she won't know up from down.

"Oh god, yes, Misha! Fuck," she spills out, her body a helpless, quivering mass as a third orgasm rolls through her. I've opened the floodgates, and she can't even hold back her own gushing words. "Just like that, please!"

I oblige her.

My thrusting keeps going with no end in sight until everything about her, the way her auburn hair is thrown back over the sheets, the way her body arches with each new orgasm, the sound of her gasping like music in the air, it's all too perfect.

When I feel another orgasm welling up in her —
I've lost count how many times she's come on my —
I let my body spill past the brink. My balls tighten,
my bucking gets less precise and wilder, random,
and my cock arches up as it prepares to unleash
on her.

White-hot pleasure shoots through my body,
paralyzing me. A full-body orgasm wracks me from
my cock to my head, and I let out one long, low
groan as my life-giving seed shoots into her hot and
fast. Pulse after pulse of it spills into her, filling her
up and spilling out over my balls and onto the
sheets.

I open my eyes to see her in the middle of her
own orgasm. Her face is so wound up it in ecstasy,
both of us just so utterly devastated by our orgasms.

Finally it ends, and we're left panting together,
my cock spilling one last spurt of seed into her
before I slowly pull out.

"Fuck," she whispers at the same time as I do, and
she giggles.

I smile down at her, stroking the side of her face
with a large hand as she opens her eyes to look up at
me lovingly.

"You," I say, "are full of surprises."

"I think you wrung the last one out of me just
then," she replies in an exhausted voice. I lean down
and kiss her softly before stepping off the bed and

stretching. I feel her eyes on me all the way to the en suite bathroom, where I take a deep breath.

That was the best sex I've had in as long as I can remember.

After I relieve myself and splash some water into my face, I decide to invite her in for a shower.

But when I push the door open, I see her peering at a glowing phone screen on my bed.

My phone.

I clear my throat, and she yelps, dropping the phone back onto my pants on the floor. Her face is red and filled with embarrassment.

"Oh! Sorry, you just got a message, and I thought it might be important."

I crack a smile at her as I approach the phone and pick it up off the floor. I glance down at the message on the screen.

Your two spies have reports ready, but the sovietnik is pinned down—we're waiting on your orders.

I glance up at her eyes. There's a hint of fear written in them, even in the bliss of her afterglow. I wonder how much of that message she understands. Her cheeks are red, but most people would be appropriately shamed for snooping.

My 'two spies' are a pair of my informants who are the eyes and ears of the *bratva,* and the sovietnik is a counselor of mine. These three men are second only to the *pakhan* in the hierarchy of the Russian mafia.

Second only to me.

But does a pretty young American stripper recognize such words?

Her face is hard to read, though. Her sweetness is as bright and full as ever, and the blush in her cheeks makes my heart melt. If she has an idea of what the text is about, she's doing a good job of hiding it, or maybe the danger excites her.

Regardless, she isn't running out the door.

"How about a shower, dove?" I ask in a husky whisper, holding my hand out and tossing the phone onto the bed, effectively offering to forget this little incident.

She hesitates, then smiles and takes my hands. "I'd like that."

I cannot believe what my life has become.

It's one in the afternoon, and I am strolling around a strip club, looking for clues. Normally, I would be dancing, but right now the club is almost totally empty. So far, I have mostly been working evening shifts, thankfully, but today one of the usual daytime dancers called out so I have been asked to come in and fill her slot.

However, there isn't much of a slot to fill.

Apparently, the noon time crowd isn't so much a crowd as just… a trickle. Mostly just bored retirees who probably go to bed at eight in the evening, so this is their prime time hours for being sleazy and stingy with the girls.

From the moment I stroll into the strip joint, it's completely obvious to me how little money there is floating around here. The high-rollers and big spenders of last night are nowhere to be found, and these old men living off disability checks and meager pensions are not cutting it.

In fact, it seems like most of them are just here to drink watered-down beer and shoot the shit with their buddies at the bar. There are only three girls working right now, including me. The other two are considerably older, both women in their forties who have kids in school.

I learned very quickly that for a lot of single mothers, this was a dream job. It let them work while their children were safely tucked away in a classroom, and when the school bell rang and they went home, their mothers could be there to help them with homework and make dinner.

Sure, the daytime shifts are nowhere near as lucrative as the night shifts, but all it takes is one generous tipper to make the day worth it. Admittedly, I went into this undercover assignment a little skeptical that I could figure out how to properly fit in with the crowd here. But after a short amount of time, I have realized that I have more in common with these women than I even expected.

I, too, often have to do things I would rather not to keep my job.

Hell, sometimes being one of the only female officers in my department feels a lot more exploitative and uncomfortable than dancing for tips. At least the men here pay me for their awkward, pervy stares and filthy comments, which is more than I can say for some of my colleagues in the vice department.

To be fair, it's kind of unusual for a woman to work in vice, especially in a high-risk, fast-paced city like Las Vegas. When I first started there, some skeezeball started a rumor that I only got the job because I blew one of our commanding officers in the bathroom.

Obviously, that was untrue. There isn't a single guy in that whole department I would even dream of touching beyond a professional handshake. It's almost funny how the vice section of Las Vegas PD is full of people who have their own vices. My old office mate was a gambler. The male secretary who files our paperwork and directs calls is often slumped over a bar counter within an hour of clocking out for the day.

As for me, I don't have a vice. And that makes me a rarity, it seems. But I have sat through far too many boring seminars on drug abuse, gambling, alcoholism, sex addiction, and all kinds of other topics to let something like that rule my life. I have a job to do, and I'll be damned if I let anything in my personal life distract me from it.

Today, though, I am starting to wonder if this is how addictions begin.

Because no matter what I do to keep my mind and body busy with work, I cannot seem to stop thinking about Misha. My brain is so focused on him, on replaying vivid imagery and scenery from our roll in the hay last night, that I keep catching myself staring off into space.

More than once, I've snapped back to reality only to notice some potential customer looking at me like I'm crazy. Earlier, when I was trying to chat up a client at the bar, I nearly slipped up and called him Misha by accident. It was a close call, saved only by the fact that my target was so old and decrepit he hardly seemed cognizant of our conversation in the first place.

All I can think about is the way the low light flickered across Misha's powerful muscles, how his eyes bored into me while his huge, strong hands guided my body. He bent me and moved me around with such ease. Before last night, it had been years since I was last even remotely intimate with anyone.

I'm only twenty-four, but the last six years of my life have been totally wrapped up in my career. Keeping up with the physical standards of the job means that I spend a ton of time at the gym, running, lifting weights, doing endless lunges and squats.

The written and oral exams I take to stay on top of my game and to get promoted mean that I spend my weekends and weeknights poring over handbooks and law books. I am always the first to ask for overtime and always the last to leave the office at the end of a shift. I jump to answer the phone. I demand more assignments than anyone else. I sign up for extra seminars and volunteer for extra responsibilities.

I'm not ashamed of the fact that I am essentially the teacher's pet of the Las Vegas vice department.

Not that my boss really acknowledges how hard I work. But that's because of one simple fact: I'm a woman. A young, decently-attractive woman. And as far as my boss is concerned, I am not the type of person who should be working at his department.

He's sexist, of course, still subscribing to the idea that vice is supposed to be a boys' club. It doesn't matter that I can run circles around my male colleagues. I have to work twice as hard to get half the recognition and respect. But it's worth it.

Or at least that's what I tell myself when the going gets tough.

But all of this means that I have had no time at all for love or romance or even sex. So my mind blowing night with Misha is getting to me a little bit. I've never been manhandled and satisfied like that before, and I might not ever again.

No, I don't have a vice. But if there was ever something I *could* get addicted to, I have a feeling it's guys like Misha. Right now, though, I have to do everything in my power to stop thinking about him. I have a job to do, and fucking him was just one small step of my elaborate plan here. I take a deep breath, smooth my hair in the dressing room mirror, apply another layer of matte burgundy lipstick, slip on my tightest, sexiest black dress, strap my feet into six-inch stiletto death traps, and walk back out onto the floor.

The lights are dim, as always, but there's something odd and off-kilter about the shadowy darkness in the middle of the bright Vegas daylight. The music is way too upbeat and up-tempo, the bass pulsing underneath my every step as I saunter across the club toward the bar. It's hard to feel sexy when you're surrounded by empty space and the coughing laughter of stingy old men, but I have to try. I plaster a smile to my face and walk up to the bar, leaning one elbow on the counter and biting my lip as I gaze down the row of men drinking beers.

"How are you boys doing today?" I pipe up, twirling a lock of auburn hair around my finger. Only two of them even look up at the sound of my voice, the other four totally engrossed in whatever sports game is playing on the TV monitor above the bar. Two out of six isn't a great average, but I will take what I can get in the middle of the day like this.

One of the guys gives me a nod, but the other just squints at me confusedly, like he's trying to figure out what I've just said. He looks a little too senile to be much of a honeypot. I decide to focus on the first guy. I give him a wink and he smiles.

"I'm good. Better now," he adds, giving me an extremely over-the-top once-over.

"Good to hear," I reply, forcing a coquettish giggle. "If you get tired of hanging around all these men, you should come and find me. I can make it worth your while."

He grins and waggles his wiry eyebrows, which very nearly makes me burst out laughing, but instead I just turn and walk away, careful to sway my hips as I leave. It's not that I really want his money or his attention, but to keep up my undercover facade, I need to be convincing. And unless I'm hustling for tips, it might look too suspicious. I don't need their money; I live a simple, modest lifestyle and I get paid a manageable wage as an officer. It's all for show, all to bolster my undercover identity.

I live in fear of the moment that one of my colleagues might come wandering into this place to blow off steam. I know them all just well enough to guess that at least a few of them venture into these seedy strip clubs on the regular. Thankfully, I haven't seen any of them yet, but if I do, there's a chance they might blow my cover. In order to make a secret, high-risk assignment like this one work, it's important to keep the circle small. In other words, almost nobody can know about it, including my coworkers.

Besides, I am not exactly thrilled at the prospect of my horn dog colleagues potentially seeing me so scantily clad. I would never be able to live it down at the office.

Abandoning the uninterested old men at the bar, I decide to do some actual police work. I mosey on up to one of the bouncers, a big, burly man with a goatee and a trilby hat. He's exactly the kind of numbskull who seems most likely to let some vital detail slip.

I've been gathering intel and waiting for the right moment to approach him for days. I sidle up to him with a sweet smile. The bouncers are used to female attention, and after months or even years of watching nearly-naked girls dance from a distance, most of them are pretty immune to our charms. But this guy seems newer than the others, which is why I've picked him.

"Hey Rob," I greet him with a little wave. His serious expression melts into a genuine smile. *Oh, this will be even easier than expected*, I think to myself.

"Hi Misty," he replies, his face going splotchy pink and white. It's still amusing to me how easily these big, buff, scary-looking bouncer guys can melt into puddles when a pretty girl shows them attention.

"Ugh, is it always this slow in the middle of the day?" I ask, leaning against the wall beside him. "There's hardly anyone here."

"Yeah, midday is usually pretty dead. Just the old dudes who come here for the cheap beer. More interested in watching football than paying for a lap dance. I think they're crazy," he admits with a sheepish grin.

"See, you understand the value of a dollar," I tease, nudging him on the arm. "Why come to a strip club just to watch a bunch of sweaty dudes throw a ball around?"

"Exactly," Rob agrees. He leans in close and adds, "But if you ask me, the real fun is underground. You know, the behind the scenes stuff."

Wow. He's cracking like an egg.

"Behind the scenes? Like, what?" I press him, batting my eyelashes innocently.

He gets a conspiratorial grin on his face and explains in a hushed tone, "You know, like the stuff they do out back. In the basement. Nobody's supposed to go down there. Not even me. Which probably means they're hiding all the, you know, the good stuff."

"Oh, really?" I remark. "What kind of stuff?"

He sighs. "Well, I don't really know. They won't let me down there. Miss Galina says it's top secret. Only certain guys get to go down there. You know what I think it is?"

"What?" I ask, egging him on. My heart races.

"Drugs," he whispers, raising both eyebrows. "Cocaine or something. Or maybe guns."

"Guns aren't drugs," I comment.

"Yeah, yeah, no. Guns *and* drugs. If I do a good

job up here I think they might let me down there sometime to see," Rob says proudly.

"Hmm. Maybe. Well, in that case, I better let you get back to work, huh?" I say brightly. Before he can even respond, I turn and walk away, a new motive in mind: to find Miss Galina and see if she's as quick to spill information as Rob was.

Galina is the house mother, the head of operations here at the strip club. She's in charge, ruling over the club with an iron fist. She can be sweet and protective over her dancers sometimes, but the bottom line is that she wants to make money. If a girl isn't pulling her weight, Galina won't hesitate to boot her. That's another reason why I've made such a concentrated effort to make money: to avoid her wrath. I need her on my side, at least long enough to pick up all the secrets this place has to hold.

And I know just where to find her. I walk back to the dressing room where the girls change clothes and put on makeup between sets. Galina has a little office on the other side of the dressing room, behind a pane of two-way glass. I learned that on my very first shift. I've spent enough time in vice to recognize a two-way mirror when I see one.

I stride through the dressing room and knock politely on her door. A few moments later, she opens it with a dubious look on her face. Galina is a short, stooped older woman with jet-black hair and dark eyes, magnified slightly through her half-moon glasses.

"Yes? What is it?" she asks, shrugging.

"Oh, I just wanted to ask you about something," I reply, suddenly nervous.

"Well, out with it," she prompts.

"I-I was just wondering if there is extra parking out back," I reply, forcing a smile. "You know, for customers. Like, is it safe for them to park behind the building? There's not any, uh, structures blocking them from doing that?"

She narrows her eyes at me, instantly suspicious. *Shit.*

"Why are you asking? There aren't enough customers here for parking to be an issue. There's plenty of space out front," Galina answers. She folds her arms over her chest. "What are you really asking? Don't you have a routine to do? Perverts to please?"

I feel my cheeks flushing pink. "Y-Yes. You're right. Sorry. I-I was just wondering. It was a stupid question, my apologies."

"You're right. It is a stupid questions," she agrees icily. "Now get back out there and make some money before all the customers go home."

"Yes, ma'am," I respond hastily. I turn on my heel and nearly run out of the dressing room, feeling like a gigantic idiot. *Slow down, Nicole. Don't get ahead of yourself,* I warn myself inwardly. *Don't blow it.*

But I can't slow down. That old burning curiosity has gotten ahold of me now. It's the same instinct that had led me to crack cases wide open in the past, and I have to ride it out to its conclusion. I've been dilly-dallying around this strip club long enough. I need to push this along.

I need to check out the underground.

On the pretense of taking a smoke break, even though I have never smoked in my life, I grab my purse and slip past Rob and the other bouncer to head outside into the bright Vegas sun. I stand quietly by the door for a moment, then when I feel the coast is clear, I slink silently around to the back of the building. My heart is pounding wildly, my blood rushing in my ears.

It's time to jump the gun.

I start searching, looking for anything that looks out of place. The strip club is in a pretty nondescript brick building, with lots of parking space out front and not much in the back. In fact, the back of the building looks pretty abandoned. It's dark, with high, unruly bushes growing over the pavement. I scan the wall for a secret door or anything out of place.

There's nothing.

But just when I'm about to give up, I take a step and hear a hollow clunk under my stiletto. I look down, squinting, to see what looks like a very frayed and weather-worn bit of cord. I glance around to make sure nobody is watching, then bend down and give it a pull.

To my horror and amazement, it opens up a small square door with a dusty staircase leading down into the ground.

"Holy shit," I murmur.

This is the kind of moment at which it's probably smart to slow down and call for backup. But that has never been my style. I like to work alone, and I can't back off now.

Without another moment of hesitation, I take off my stilettos and climb down the short staircase and into a dank, musty basement, closing the trap door behind me. The dust and grime is so thick I can hardly see, until I use my cell phone to light the way. I see unmarked crates stacked all the way to the ceiling, and I know without even having to check that this is contraband of some sort.

This is a hustle. An illegal one. A massive payload I should not handle alone.

I break down and call the department, quietly telling them to send squad cars. Just as I hang up, I hear a scuffling above. I look up at the door to see it pulling open!

"Shit," I whisper, and shimmy in behind a tall stack of heavy crates to hide as my heart hammers away in my chest. I can't get caught down here!

Moments later, a tall, hulking figure comes down

the stairs. Heavy footsteps. A familiar scent... cologne.

I peek to see who or what has entered the basement, and I nearly gasp out loud. It's Misha, dressed in a tailored suit and carrying another crate, which he sets down on a stack. He checks his cell phone in the darkness, his eyes locked on the screen. I'm too afraid to breathe, much less move.

If he sees me, I could be dead. And who knows how long I will have to wait here until backup arrives. I stare at him, sizing him up. I don't see a gun in his hands or pockets, and his suit jacket is too neatly tailored to hide any large bulges.

So, he's unarmed. But so am I, and his muscular body dwarfs mine.

And then, the worst happens: I inhale too much dust.

I try to resist, my face screwing up, my eyes beginning to water. I beg my body not to betray me, to keep my place a secret, but I can't fight it any longer. I sneeze, trying to silence the noise as best I can, but it's no use.

Within seconds, Misha is on me, staring me down with those blazing blue eyes. I can scarcely breathe, but I'm determined to stay strong. I can't show weakness.

The recognition in his eyes makes my heart skip a beat.

"Misty?" he murmurs, frowning. "What the hell are you doing here?"

"I-I was, um…" I trail off awkwardly. Then I realize there's no point in trying to make it coy. He will see right through me. I straighten up and reply, "You've been hiding a lot down here, it looks like. What is your full name, Misha?"

He glares at me, his jaw tightening. I glance at his hands, which are surprisingly not balled into fists. It's like he's doing everything in his power to hold back.

"Misha Chaykovsky," he answers in a calm, low growl.

"Well, then," I begin, trying to stay tough. "Misha Chaykovsky, you are under arrest."

He doesn't budge. He's radiating pure rage and betrayal, but there's something else there, too. Genuine pain. Hurt. I almost feel guilty, even though I know logically he is the bad guy, not me. So why do I feel so awful?

And why isn't he fighting back? Most men would have killed me already. But Misha is just standing in front of me, stoic and still. It occurs to me as clear as day: he won't hurt me. Even though I am about to arrest him and destroy his life, he won't lay a hand on me. There is some unspoken code of honor that prevents him from doing so, even though he so easily could.

"You have the right to remain silent," I begin

quietly, watching his face. "Anything you say can and will be used against you in a court of—"

BANG! The door above us is flung open and several heavily-armed officers from vice come pouring into the basement. It only takes seconds before they're clinking handcuffs over Misha's wrists, dragging him into custody as I watch open-mouthed, in shock at how quickly it's all unfolding.

Throughout the entire ordeal, Misha never says a single word. One of my colleagues claps me on the shoulder and drapes a robe around me to cover my half-naked body, but I can hardly even respond. I did it. I cracked the case. I got the man arrested. I should be proud.

And yet, why do I feel so awful?

I hear the sound of the air the inmate's fist cuts as I move my head back just enough to dodge his wild punch. His second blow comes in and connects with my gut, but I tense my muscles before impact and barely feel a thing.

The kid squaring off against me in the rec yard doesn't know what he's getting into.

He's in his early twenties with a shaved head, broad shoulders, tattoos up his neck, and a chip on his shoulder. He'd be intimidating to many other people, but to me, he's just another one of the young punks constantly trying to get the upper hand on me.

He's just another gray face.

Everything in here is gray. Gray walls, gray floors, gray ceilings, gray people, and a gray future.

I can see the mountains just barely over the

concrete walls, and they're so distant and fuzzy that they might as well not be real. They're just props to make us think we're still part of the world we were snatched away from.

My attacker lunges in again, and I twist away to the side, keeping my hands far from him. This time, his hardened knuckle grazes my brow, and I feel a slight sting.

A drop of red falls from the cut to the gray concrete beneath us.

I feel like I'm a bullfighter. The kid charges in time after time, but I just keep twisting away from him. Other inmates gathered around us, both to clear a space and to gawk.

There are Russians here in the detention center. They know me, and they respect me, but every time one of them starts to come in to my defense, I hold out a hand to keep him back.

In about ten seconds, the guards are going to be all over us, and I don't plan on either me or my comrades spending a single second in solitary.

The attacker comes low and tries to go for my legs, but I slide back and let him fall to the ground, scraping his chin on the concrete. There's a ripple of laughter from the men around us, and I put my hands on my hips and smile down at him while he scowls at me and pushes himself up.

"You'd be dead right now, if we weren't behind bars," I say patiently. "You're welcome."

"Fuck you, Russky," he spits back, and I soundly dodge another punch.

"I'm not the one you want to be worrying about," I grunt back. "They are."

The next second, no less than five guards descend on us, whistles blowing in our ears and nightsticks coming out. As I expected, three of them tackle me to the ground, while two take down my attacker. The rest of the crowd breaks up as I let myself be apprehended by the guards. Once I'm on the ground, a boot pressed into my back, I exchange a silent nod with one of the Russians making eye contact with me.

He nods in return, and they disperse.

I'm hauled back to my cell, saying not a word and making no move to resist. If I wanted to, I could kill all three of my guards without a second thought. So many times as they march me down the bleak hallways, I see moments where I could wrestle my way free and get a weapon from one of them.

It's my training kicking in from the Special Forces. I can read so much as a change in the way I'm being held as a weakness to be exploited. I have to hold myself back from it.

The system is looking for me to slip up so I can lose my one chance at getting out of here, and I'm not going to give them that satisfaction.

Within minutes, I'm back in my box of a cell, and the door gets slammed behind me with a clatter. I stand there a few moments, glaring at a chip in the ceiling before I slowly stride over to the bed and sit down on it.

There's a lot more waiting in jail than you expect. Sitting, waiting, thinking. Some would call it meditating, but I've never been about that kind of thing.

It's just time to either sharpen the mind or let it rot.

Sometime later, I watch the lines of inmates walk past my cell as recreation time ends. The guy who picked a fight for me while I was trying to work out is gone, probably hauled off to seg. It was obvious to everyone that he started the fight, and I made a point not to fight back. He ended up looking like a punk, and I looked untouchable.

And as the kid's skinhead friends eye me furiously as they march by, I know just how valuable it is to seem untouchable in here.

Incarceration turns good men into animals. Rising above that is a feat.

I've had few times in my life where I need to hold back unbridled anger, so practicing this now has been a... unique experience.

Every cell of my mind wants to focus all its fury on that one damn cop who put me in here.

Nicole Burns.

The name hovers over me. I could almost laugh at the fact that it's an appropriate name, considering how badly she burned me. Or maybe that the name has been burned into my mind since she first pulled that badge on me.

Everything about her is infuriating, in hindsight. That act as a stripper, the fake name, the fake personality... and she even had the gall to ride her cover all the way to my bedroom.

The best sex of my life, with a cop. I smiled darkly and ran a hand through my hair. She really likes playing with the dragon's fire, doesn't she?

Time for dinner rolls around, and a guard lets me out of my cell to march me to the mess hall, where the sea of men is already getting seated with trays of gray food. I go through the line with the other men, making no small talk before I make my way to my table and take a seat.

Some of the other Russian inmates gather around me, giving me respectful nods of their heads before I grant them a seat. Even behind bars, I command their respect. They know their *pakhan*, even if they weren't part of my organization on the outside.

"The man who came after you in the exercise yard, he's been put in solitary," says the first man to sit down across from me. Within a minute, we have a table full of Russians. There is strength in numbers.

"Good," I grunt.

"We're already planning to retaliate," he goes on, exchanging nods with a few of the others. "The skinheads normally stick together, but two of them break off to go jogging every other day, and-"

"No," I say simply, and the men are silenced, blinking in confusion.

"Sir, this is an attack on our reputation," one of the bigger men to my right explains respectfully. "If they sense weakness, they will strike first."

"When you are strong, let your enemies think you are weak, and when you are weak, let them think you are strong," I reply in a cool, even tone. "We are Russians, not warhawks. You are fine men, and I see how you stick together. If some white supremacist trash wants to prod a sleeping bear, *then* you will swipe back. But do so slowly, and only when you know it will devastate them."

The men nod to me respectfully, seeing the wisdom in my words. They served me well on the outside, and I plan to run a tight ship as long as I'm in.

The chatter of the people all around us is loud, but surprising as it sounds, this kind of public environment is one of the few moments we have to speak in private. Here and in the rec yard — crowds offer privacy to talk, because when you're alone, the guards have ears everywhere.

"Now," I say after I've had a few moments to attack my food. "About this police officer, this Nicole Burns."

The men lean forward, interested. Word of my arrest spread quickly, but I've been relatively silent on the issue.

"Sir, if I may," the same large man says, and I raise an eyebrow at him, but nod. "I have a contact on the outside who may be able to pull strings for us and have her dealt with. He is not a man of your caliber, but he can get the job done in such a way that it looks like an accident — not a murder, but an injury that can't be traced to us but will still send a message, if she's paying attention.

"You will not lay a finger on her," I say calmly yet firmly, and again, my men are surprised. I have a fatherly love for my soldiers, but they are blood-thirsty.

"Sir?"

"Do not let this place give you a taste for petty revenge," I explain. "That kind of behavior will make you look like the rabid beast the guards want you to be."

Even as I say the words, I feel the restraint cutting into me. I've had my best men try to back-stab me and fail, but no betrayal has felt so bitter as Nicole's. After that night we shared together, I thought I was seeing a woman in a way I'd never seen one before, but she turned all that into ash in my mouth.

Still, I would stick to this tactic, because as much as I hate to admit it to myself... she's my only way out of here.

"Nicole Burns," I say, my eyes panning around to each and every man present, "is the only witness to the evidence that got me arrested. As the arresting officer, her word is golden." The men nod, following along. "But she had plenty of opportunity to make a move on me earlier than that, and she never did. I think this Nicole Burns is more than meets the eye."

"You think someone could sway her?" my acting advisor suggests, stroking his chin, and I give a single, slow nod.

"She may be pliable. Her testimony is what will entirely determine whether I'm sentenced properly." I make eye contact with each and every man at the table. "I am not deaf, either — I know there are rumors of plots against me on the outside. If I stay here, my position may be shaken, and I may be replaced with some ambitious young fuck who couldn't care less about you all. As for me, you know I have never failed to support my comrades behind bars."

It's not a lie. I've kept informants and supply chains close to the Nevada prison system for years, and the looks on the faces of the men around me tells me they're grateful.

"So we need to contact the officer, preferably with a sweet deal," my advisor says.

"Exactly," I say. I glance past one of my men to the skinheads at the table across the cafeteria. They're like devils chattering to each other. "If we need to make the deal even sweeter, we may be able to offer leverage against the skinheads. Two birds, one stone."

The men seem to like this plan, and they murmur approval amongst themselves.

"Dmitri, you get word out to your contacts about wanting to meet with our Officer Burns. Nikolai, put some pressure on one of the rats around here and see what you can get him to squeal about that the police might like. The rest of you, be on your guard." The men nod at my orders, and we finish our dinner in good spirits.

I'm on my way back to my cell when Dmitri catches up to me. "Comrade," he says, glancing over his shoulder. "If your mind is on a coup from the outside, we should be wary putting pressure on the skinheads. They're known to carry out hits for the highest bidder, and you're still new."

"Let them come," I say simply. "One of two things will happen. Either this plan will work and I'll be out before a hit can make its way in, or I'll be locked away long enough that a little time in solitary won't kill me." I crack a wicked grin over my shoulder at him. "A few years is worth a dead skinhead, don't you think?"

I'm only half-joking.

We make our way back to our cells, but there's a guard waiting by mine. At first, I worry that our talk at the table has already made it to the guards, but the man's face doesn't read as such.

"Chaykovsky," he addresses me curtly by my last name, "you've got a visitor. Do you accept?"

I'm surprised, but my face doesn't shift to give it away. "Who is it?" I ask.

The guard frowns and looks at the little card in his hand, squinting at the name before he replies.

"Nicole Burns."

This is not the way I ever pictured this mission to go. Not in a million years. Sure, I have caught the bad guy, or at least one of the bad guys, but it doesn't feel as satisfying as I anticipated when I first got this assignment.

I sat through months of planning and strategizing to make this happen. Undercover missions are never simple. It takes time to build a proper alias, to sketch out the necessary details that could be the difference between life and death. It really is that dire, especially when the assignment involves the mafia.

If anyone at the club had caught wind of my true identity, I would have been in imminent danger. Not every cop can handle the stress and sacrifice of going undercover. For most of us, it means leaving or barely seeing our families and friends. It means being alienated and isolated from your usual life, from everything you know and love, for as long as the mission takes.

Many of the guys in my department have families. Wives, young children, a domestic life they can't just drop and abandon while they go off on some risky mission with a fake identity.

But me? I am the perfect candidate for these missions. I don't really have a family to speak of, and I definitely don't have a husband or children.

All I have is my little sister, Samantha. We are fairly close, talking on the phone every few days or so. But she's a college sophomore, living all the way in San Francisco. She's an eight-hour drive away, and besides, Sam has her own life, her own circle of friends who surround her and support her out in California.

That's not to say she doesn't still love her sister; the two of us have relied on each other for years, especially after what happened with Mom. But she doesn't visit home very often, and I can hardly blame her. Both of us have some less than pleasant memories here, and I'm happy that Sam got to go to California to escape the gloom and constant reminders of the past.

So, without anyone here in Vegas to depend on me or look after me, I'm kind of mostly alone. My career is the love of my life at the moment, and I made it that way on purpose. I have been independent for a long time, and I'm definitely not afraid of hard work and sacrifice.

When my superior officer offered me the opportunity to go undercover, I jumped at the chance. I have been angling for a career-building shot like this for years, and I was more than ready to take it on.

I simply told Samantha I was going out of town and would be unavailable for a while, which she accepted without hesitation or question. I sat through the strategy meetings, psychological testing, and security briefings like a champ. Did I look forward to posing as a stripper? No. Not really. I have always been in great shape, but I have never considered myself much of a dancer, and I don't think of myself as a seductive woman. But I got into character by necessity, pulled it off without so much as a hiccup, and in the end, I got Misha Chaykovsky in handcuffs.

A job well done, right?

Not so much, according to my boss. I came into the office this morning expecting a little bit of fanfare, or at least some high-fives and a welcome back. But it's almost as though nobody even noticed I was gone all that time.

Weeks of undercover work passed by, and nobody cares. I am currently sitting in my office cubicle, staring wide-eyed at the massive stack of paperwork piled on top of my cherry wood desk. I thought at least some of this could be passed off to someone else. You know, someone who wasn't on a top-secret, very important undercover mission to take down the mafia bigwigs in this city, and therefore a little bit distracted from the humdrum cycle of paperwork and filing.

But no. Nobody covered me at all, it seems.

"Wonderful," I sigh to myself as I begin picking through the stack and sorting papers. And to make matters worse, there is a sticky note on my computer monitor with a message scrawled in my boss's nearly illegible chicken scratch.

COME SEE ME ASAP.

"What the hell did I do now?" I groan, rolling my eyes. I don't suppose there is a chance in hell he might just want to congratulate me on completing the mission and making the arrest. I get up, push my swivel chair in, and head down the hall to my boss's office.

It's a much bigger, fancier room than mine, with a gorgeous wide window that allows a panoramic view of the Vegas skyline. It is truly beautiful. It feels kind of like a travesty that a man like Lieutenant Harden gets to sit in this office. It's too good for him, in my opinion. Of course, I keep that opinion very much to myself. The lieutenant already doesn't like me much.

I knock on the office door and wait for an answer.

"Come on in," barks Lieutenant Harden. I push

the door open and step inside, giving him a tentative smile. When he sees that it's me, he gets a smarmy look on his face and leans back in his chair, regarding me with narrowed eyes and a smirk.

"Yes, Lieutenant? You wanted to see me?" I greet him, trying hard not to fidget. Something about the way he looks at me always makes my skin crawl. It's like he's not seeing me in my uniform, but… in lingerie, or something. It's gross.

"Yeah. I did. So, you're back," he remarks. I nod.

"Yes, sir. Mission completed," I comment, a little proudly.

"I wouldn't be so quick to congratulate myself if I were you," Harden begins. I can feel my face blushing as my smile fades. "You didn't follow protocol. And you took your damn time, too. You're lucky you made it out of there alive. And with your career intact."

"I beg your pardon, Sir, but—"

"But nothing," he interrupts, holding up both hands. "You screwed up, Officer Burns. You went about this the wrong way altogether."

"What exactly did I do wrong?" I ask, starting to feel a little pissed off. The lieutenant sighs heavily.

"Well, you entered the basement of the club without backup. You blew your cover down there almost immediately, without inspecting what was in the crates. You attempted to arrest our target without backup and without handcuffs. And if we think back a little further, I have to admit, it seems like you might have enjoyed your fake identity a little too much, Burns," he explains, shrugging. My mouth falls open.

"Excuse me?" I ask, breathless.

"Oh, you heard me," Harden says. He leans forward and lowers his voice. "I thought you would make a good stripper, but I didn't think you'd warm up to the job so quickly. And, uh, *thoroughly*," he adds pointedly.

"What are you talking about?" I press him, trying to remain calm.

"Thank god I sent one of the guys to keep tabs on you at that sleazy strip joint. He saw you go home with the gangster. Like some common whore. You do know what we really mean by 'getting close to your target,' right? It doesn't mean you sleep with him," he insinuates.

My heart sinks. "I-I didn't. I didn't do anything," I murmur tensely.

"Yes, you did. And whatever it was, you must have done a pretty good job. With that part, at least. Maybe you'd make a better whore than a vice cop. We all got our demons, Burns, but I didn't expect yours to be big, burly Russian gangsters. I could fire you right here, right now," he sneers. Then he leans back in his chair, fixing me with a critical eye. "But you know how we can smooth this over, right?"

"How?" I ask desperately. "I'll do anything."

Harden grins smugly.

"Oh, I bet you will."

It dawns on me what he's hinting at and I take a horrified step back.

"What? No. You're kidding me. I would never," I retort, wrinkling my nose in disgust.

"Ha. Don't act so innocent now, Burns. Compared to whatever you did with that Russian rat, a night with me should be a walk in the park," he chuckles, steepling his fingers.

I stare at him silently for a moment, then decide it's time to just leave. I can't deal with this right now. My brain can't even compute what he's saying to me.

"I have paperwork to do," I tell him. I turn and march out of his office and back to my desk, my heart hammering away. How dare he? How disgusting! I pull up my email and start typing up a message to Harden's superior, to turn him in for propositioning me at work.

But then I remember that Harden is up for a promotion soon, and with the way this sexist department works, there's no question about the fact that he will get it. And when he does, he'll have even more power to make my life miserable.

I delete the email draft.

I need to distract myself. I start poring over the statements and details regarding Misha's arrest, and it doesn't take me too long to discover a small discrepancy in the timeline.

"Shit," I mutter to myself. God, all of my colleagues here are useless. Do I really have to do everything myself? I know that if I don't get this detail fixed, it will be my ass on the line.

Chaykovsky is my arrest, and I'm the one that has to dot all the i's and cross all the t's.

Besides, I need to get the hell out of this office for a while anyway.

I pack up my stuff and tell the secretary I'm heading out for an interview. I climb into my car and take off in the direction of the detention center where I know my "Russian gangster" is being held.

It's a long drive, long enough to let my mind wander. Which, at the moment, is a dangerous move. I can't stop thinking about how shitty my boss is. I can't believe he would do this to me. Not only tear me apart for carrying out my mission and making the arrest the only way I knew how, but to proposition me.

To try and blackmail me into having sex with him.

I never thought I would end up in a situation like this. Ever since I was a little girl, the only thing I ever wanted to do was become a police officer, just like my father. When I was growing up, it was my dad I felt closest to. He and I just clicked, and I was a total daddy's girl. He was my best friend, the one I confided my secrets in, the one I turned to whenever I was hurt or scared.

My father was a patient, loving, hard-working man who inspires me even to this day, years and years after his tragic death. He worked as a small-town cop in a town outside of Las Vegas, where I grew up. It's a quiet suburb, where crime is almost unheard of. Not like the city, which is crawling with criminal activity. The vision of my father in his uniform, coming home from work with a tired smile on his face comforts me even now. I used to wait by the front door when it was time for his shift to end, and as soon as his car pulled into the driveway, I would run out to meet him.

He would scoop me up into his arms and swing me around, asking me about my day. He was full of funny and harrowing stories from his job, and even though his career wore him out, he always had energy to play with me and listen to me talk at the end of the day.

"I miss you, Dad," I mutter to myself as I roll along down the desert highway. "What the hell would you tell me to do in this situation? I wish you could tell me."

I have tried my hardest to follow in his footsteps, but being a big city cop is worlds away from being a police officer in a small, cozy suburb. Besides, I am a woman, working in vice, with no one to stand up for me. My boss can do whatever he wants and I have no recourse. How can I fight back when there's no one around to back me up?

I can't lose this job, though. I want to make my father proud. I can't disgrace his memory by being fired, or worse: quitting the force. He was the kind of man who never gave up, and I am determined to be just like him.

I just have to figure out a way around this. If that means I have to interview Misha Chaykovsky every day until all the details are right and the case I'm building against him is immaculate, then so be it.

Deep down, a voice at the back of my mind asks if that's the only reason I want to see him, and a flash of memory of our amazing night together hits me full force. I have to blink it away, taking in several deep breaths to steady myself again.

I'm a professional. Sleeping with him might not have been the best way to get what I wanted, but I couldn't turn down the opportunity to get close to my target.

When I arrive at the detention center, I'm full of fire and determination. It doesn't take me long to get through the security measures, chatting with the guards and staff as I make my way through. The worst part of the whole ordeal is just walking through the rows of inmates in their cells, men who are starved for female attention. They shout and holler horrible names and threats my way, calling me every curse word under the sun, grabbing their crotches, sexually propositioning me in a more...

direct fashion than the insinuation Lieutenant Harden made.

I just keep my head held high and march right through to the secure little room where I will meet with Misha. When I walk in, he's already sitting there, his feet and wrists chained to the table. He regards me with a totally unreadable expression, his blue eyes cold and hard as a glacier.

In contrast, I can feel my body warming up instantly, responding to the sight of him. He's like a magnet, drawing me closer. Even in his orange jumpsuit, he's easily the hottest man I have ever had the fortune — or misfortune — of meeting. It seems like they couldn't quite find a big enough jumpsuit for him. His muscles bulge and strain underneath the scratchy orange fabric.

"You have fifteen minutes," the guard informs me. "We'll stay nearby, don't worry. If you need anything or if he gives you any trouble, just yell."

"Got it. Thank you," I reply. The guard leaves and I take my seat at the table across from Misha, who is still sitting silently. He doesn't even seem angry, just… cold.

"Good afternoon," I tell him, clearing my throat awkwardly. I take out my paperwork and spread it across the table, then click open my pen. I look back up at him. "I need to ask you some questions regarding your whereabouts three days ago."

"Ask away," he replies flatly.

"On the morning of the 19th, where were you?" I ask.

"Was that the morning after the night we spent together?" Misha responds.

I blush immediately.

"No, that was — that was a different morning."

Something close to a smile flickers across his face.

"You weren't even afraid of me that day in the basement. You stood up to me like you were invincible," he muses aloud. Those icy blue eyes never break away from me for a moment.

"I was doing my job," I answer quietly. "And... I *was* afraid."

He gives me a slow, approving nod. "You hid it well."

"And you didn't hurt me, even though you could have," I add, frowning in confusion.

He shrugs. "You're a woman. I would never lay a hand on a woman unless she specifically asked me to. I think you remember that."

I'm getting flustered now, trying to dodge the sparks flying between us, the memories burned into my mind.

"Could you just answer the questions? You said you would."

"No. I said you could ask. I didn't say anything about actually answering," Misha explains coolly. I heave a sigh.

"Please," I lean forward, lowering my voice. "Look, my boss is giving me a lot of grief and I just need to get these facts straight."

"So, because your boss is an asshole, you want me to help you incriminate me further?" he asks, smiling. I realize with a jolt how stupid I'm being. Of course he isn't going to help me.

"No. You're right. That makes sense. I'm sorry for — ugh, why am I apologizing? You're the criminal here, not me," I groan. "If you're not going to answer my questions, then—"

"You were one hell of an actress," Misha interrupts. "But just between you and me, you seemed a lot happier as a stripper than you are as a cop."

I blanched.

"I'm not a stripper. And what I did with you — what we did together — that was wrong. That was stupid. A mistake on my part."

"Didn't feel like a mistake to me," he says, his heavy shoulders lifting into a shrug, the chains rattling against the table.

"Even though it led to your arrest?" I ask, tilting my head to one side.

He smirks. "Let's not pretend like our night together did anything to solidify your case against me. You could have done just as well without sleeping with me. You didn't even have to meet me to arrest me in the basement. Didn't even need to be a stripper for that. Could have just gotten a warrant if you suspected criminal activity in that club."

"Ah-ah-ah, keep your voice down, please," I shush him, glancing around nervously.

He chuckles. "Look, *Misty*, you're in a jail right now. Do you really think anyone here gives a damn that we spent the night together? Far worse things go on behind bars every day."

"My name's not Misty," I tell him, without thinking. "My name is Nicole Burns."

"Nicole," he repeats, nodding slowly. "That suits you much better."

"So, are you going to answer my questions or not? I have a lot to—" I trail off as my cell phone starts ringing. "Just a second," I say, getting up and walking away to check my phone.

It's not a number I recognize. Frowning, I answer. "Officer Burns."

"Nicole Burns?" asks the curt female voice.

"Yes. That's me. Can I ask who's calling?"

"I'm with the San Francisco PD, calling to inform you that your sister, Samantha Burns, has recently been reported missing by her college roommate."

My heart stops for a second. "What? Excuse me?"

"Yes, ma'am. You are Samantha's next of kin, correct?"

"Yes, I am. What happened? Where did she go?" I demand, starting to feel weak in the knees. This cannot be happening.

"Well, we don't know yet, ma'am. This is just a call to let you know."

"It's Officer. Officer Burns," I correct her. "Please tell me what you know."

"What happened?" asks a deep male voice from across the room. In my state of distress I forgot that Misha was even here. I glance over at him to see that he looks genuinely concerned, which doesn't make sense. He hardly knows me. And what little he does know of me can't possibly mean he likes me very much. After all, I am the whole reason why he's being bars right now. But when I glare at him, he sits back down, a solemn expression on his handsome face.

"Ma'am," she says, undermining my title once more, "there isn't much information for me to give you at this time. We will call you if we hear anything further. Goodbye."

"No, no. Don't go. Please, I need more information! Something. Anything. What do the police think happened? How long has she been missing? Is she hurt?" I ramble, pressing my hand to my chest. I can feel my heart fluttering a million miles a minute.

"Miss— Officer Burns, I wish I had something more to tell you," the woman sighs in more annoyance than compassion. "I understand how stressful this must be."

"Stressful? Excuse me, but no, you do not understand what I am feeling right now!" I exclaim, tears starting to burn in my eyes. "You couldn't possibly understand. Is your sister missing, too?"

There was a moment of silence and I laid my face in my palm, sighing in frustration. "Look, I'm sorry," I tell her quietly. "I'm just worried, that's all. I know you're just doing your job. It's not your fault."

"It's fine. I don't blame you for getting emotional. I can't even begin to imagine what's going through your head right now," she replies, in a much more sympathetic tone. "But just try not to overthink this too much yet, okay? If I can be frank with you, people go missing all the time, and nine times out of ten, they come back on their own. Now, your sister is a bright young woman, I expect. She's a student, right?"

"Yes," I answer, a lump forming in my throat. "She's studying to be an artist."

"So that means she has classes to attend, home-work to do, papers to write. She has a routine. She has a life here. If she's gone missing, she's got a thou-sand reasons to come home," the woman explains slowly.

"No, but that's the thing. She wouldn't just leave like that," I protest, shaking my head.

"Who? What is going on?" pipes up Misha. I give him another silencing glare, but he just watches me with those stony blue eyes. I know there's no chance that I am going to finish this interview. I have to get out of here. My priorities have shifted. I'm not inter-ested in getting the facts straight for my case.

I need to find my sister.

"Sometimes young people can be hard to predict, but it sounds like you and your sister are very close. Hopefully she will reach out soon. Keep in touch and we will update you if there are any new develop-ments in the case. Try to stay calm."

"Thank you," I tell her quickly before hanging up and sliding the phone back into my pocket. I look over at Misha, who hasn't taken his eyes off of me this whole time.

"You're upset. Something happened. Something personal," he says grimly.

"Yeah, good guess," I shoot back, a little more viciously than I meant to. Misha seems totally unperturbed by my sarcastic response, though. He still just looks worried.

About me.

Why?

"This interview is over. I will get back to you and we will finish this... soon. I have to go now," I tell him hastily. "Guard!"

The same guard as before comes hurrying back. "Is there an issue? Is he giving you any trouble, Officer?" he asks, leaning around to glare at Misha over my shoulder.

"No, no. He's fine. It's fine. I just have to leave. Something… something has come up," I explain, forcing a polite smile to hurry things along. "I'm sorry to have wasted your time. I just need to get out of here."

"Of course. No problem, Officer Burns," the guard says, sliding the bars so I can get out. As I stride away from him as fast as I can go without actually running, he calls out after me, "Hey! Tell your lieutenant I said hi!"

"Sure!" I call back, rolling my eyes.

I all but dash down through the rows of inmates, ignoring them as they all shout and whistle and catcall me lewdly from their cells. Right now, I couldn't care less about them. Any of them. The only thing that matters to me right now is Samantha and making sure she's okay.

I rush out of the detention center, fidgeting my way through security, and burst out into the desert sunshine. I jog across the parking lot and fiddle with the car keys to unlock the driver's side door, my hands trembling so badly I can hardly stick the key in the hole.

"Fuck," I mutter to myself, annoyed at how my body's nervousness is betraying me right now, when I need to move quickly. Finally, I manage to open the door and slide behind the wheel, jamming the key into the ignition. I have a terrible ache in the pit of my stomach as I peel out of the parking lot and back onto the dusty highway. I turn off the music and stare straight ahead down the flat road, watching the little blurry mirage of water dancing in the distance.

It makes me think of long car rides with my family as a little girl. Sam and I used to point out the watery mirage shimmering down the road and tell our parents they were going to drive through a big puddle, only to watch with awe and disappointment when we got closer and the shimmer disappeared.

It was an almost magical phenomenon to me as a

little girl. Sam and I could never quite figure out why such an illusion could occur, but we didn't question it too much. Life was amazing back then, and the idea of a magical illusion dancing along on the open desert road wasn't too hard to believe in.

Nowadays, I find it hard to believe in any kind of miracle. Life is hard, and the magic has more or less been power washed away by the harsh reality of adulthood. I work twice as hard to get half the recognition as my male colleagues. I throw every ounce of effort and energy into my job, so that at the end of the day, there's nothing left for myself. And for the most part, I have accepted that without too much issue. After all, I have convinced myself that my line of work is important, that I help make the world a better place. A safer place.

But right now, I feel completely fucking helpless. I couldn't even protect my own sister from something terrible happening.

I know in my heart Sam didn't just get up and leave of her own accord. She may be a free spirit, considerably less of a workaholic than I am, but she's not reckless or irresponsible. She loves her classes and her friends. She pays her own bills, even though I pay her tuition and send her extra money to help out when I can. Samantha isn't some empty-headed drifter who would just drop everything and abandon her life in San Francisco.

No.

If she's missing… it's because somebody took her.

And that is why I am driving to the airport.

If there is one thing in this world I care about more than my career, it's family. And right now, the only family I have is Samantha. She's the only person in this world who truly cares about me, and I'll be damned if I just sit back and watch the San Francisco police department treat her like a runaway case.

"She wouldn't do that," I murmur under my breath. "Sam isn't a runaway."

I don't have a solid plan. Not yet. All I can think to do is buy a plane ticket, whatever it costs, and fly out to California to start investigating this case myself. I may be a cop, and that may mean that I should put my trust in other police departments to handle cases on their own.

But instead, it's just made me more suspicious and wary of other departments. How do I know that the San Fran PD is going to actually look into Sam's case properly? It sounds like they've already dismissed her case as a simple runaway scenario. Strike one against them. I can't trust them to do this right. Nobody cares about her the way I do, and that means nobody will investigate her whereabouts as thoroughly as I can.

I throw the car into the next gear and floor it. At

this point, I don't even care if I'm speeding like a bat out of hell. This is my baby sister we're talking about. I need to be on the next flight out of town. I need to get there as soon as possible.

My phone starts ringing at top volume and I nearly jump out of my skin.

"Holy shit," I swear, glancing over at the cell phone buzzing on the passenger seat. I grab it and answer hastily, pressing the phone against my ear.

"Hello? Is this the San Francisco police department? Do you have more information about my sister?" I rattle off, my voice shaking.

There's a crackling sound through the phone and I frown in confusion. There's a clicking. Like the call is being recorded. *What the hell*? I worry that maybe I just don't have very good reception out here in the desert.

"Hello? Hello? Is anyone there?" I ask impatiently.

"Nicole Burns," growls a rough voice. It's soft and gravelly, with that crackling noise overlaid. The voice sounds muffled, as though someone is holding their hand over the phone while they speak.

"Yes. That's me. Who the hell is this?" I demand.

"The answer to your question," the man replies. There's a slight accent to his words, and it's almost familiar, but not quite. It's infuriating.

"Excuse me? Is this a prank call? I don't have time for this right now," I retort, about to hang up and toss the phone in the back seat. But before I do, the voice says something that makes my blood run cold.

"Where is Samantha?" hisses the voice.

I nearly run the car off the road, struggling to regain composure.

"What did you just say? Who is this?" I ask breathlessly.

"That is your question, *yea?*"

"What do you know about my sister? Who's calling? What the hell is going on?" I reply, tears starting to sting in my eyes.

"I am the answer," he continues on, just as calmly as before. "I know where she is."

"Then tell me, you fucking asshole! Where is my sister?" I shout into the phone.

"Patience, Officer."

"Screw patience, what did you do with Samantha?" I snap.

"Nothing. Yet."

The *yet* gives me pause and makes my stomach churn.

"Are you… are you threatening her? What is this? What do you want from me?" I ask tearfully. I can hear what sounds like another voice in the background, a more familiar one, though I can't place how.

"Money," is the simple reply.

"Money," I repeat in a whisper. "You want money. How much money? How much do you want?"

I can barely get the words out now. It feels like all the air has been kicked out of my lungs. Has someone really kidnapped my little sister for ransom? There is no way this can be happening to me.

"Four million dollars," answers the man coolly.

"Four million. Are you fucking kidding me?" I shoot back. "You seem to know I'm an officer, yes? So you know I don't get paid anywhere near enough to have that kind of money."

"Hmm. Perhaps," he replies.

I'm stunned into silence for a moment, a thousand thoughts ricocheting around in my head. He doesn't even seem worried about the fact that I don't have the money. It dawns on me that it isn't actually money he's after. It's something else.

But what, I don't know.

"Is there anything else I can do? I don't have the money. You know I don't. But please, please, don't hurt her. I'll do anything," I beg of him.

"You love your sister, hm?"

"Yes! Of course, I love my sister. Don't you lay a hand on her! Oh god. Put her on the line. I need to hear her voice and know that she's okay. Please. Just let me talk to her for a second," I whimper, the tears rolling down my cheeks.

"You will do anything to save her?"

"Obviously, yes. She's my baby sister. Shit, just let me hear her voice," I beg.

"You don't have the money."

"No. I don't. But I can give you something else," I protest, unable to think clearly.

"What would you give?" he asks calmly.

I wrack my brain for an answer, but come up empty.

"I don't know. I'm sorry, please, please... I can't think of anything right now, but there's got to be something—"

"If you want to see your sister again," he begins flatly, with a second voice chattering in the background, "You will find something. And Nicole... no cops."

Click.

"No. No, no, no," I mutter, looking at the phone screen. *Call ended*, it reads.

"No!" I scream, desperately thumbing over to my recent call log to check the number. It was a blocked number, no way to call back or track it. Gone, without a trace. I'm no closer to finding out what's happened to my sister. I immediately start to dial the number for the San Francisco police department, but then I stop myself, remembering the man's final words.

No cops.

I'm on my own.

And it occurs to me that the accent I struggled to place sounded awfully close to Russian. And it wasn't 'yea', he'd said... It was *da.*

I slam on the brakes and whip the car around in a massive U-turn, hurtling back in the direction I came from. Toward the detention center. Where the only man I think might be able to help me is sitting behind bars.

Because I put him there.

Keeping business under control from behind bars is a delicate ordeal.

I lift my torso up, feeling the burn in my abs as I do a full sit-up while hanging by my legs from one of the bars in the exercise yard. My handful of Russians are standing nearby me, another of them working out while the rest stand watch. Exercise keeps me centered while I'm here. It also gives me time to think without looking suspicious.

It isn't just the guards I have to be mindful of while I'm in here.

This detention center houses enough Russians that we can all stand in one corner and know each other on a first-name basis. On top of that, I'm an outsider, even if I command respect among my men. In a state prison or federal penitentiary, there are long-term inmates, set channels and hierarchy, and groups that don't move around very quickly.

This is nothing like that.

Most people are only here for a short time. Misdemeanors get out with a fine. Everyone else gets transferred out within forty-six days. That means that the jail population of about four thousand is constantly changing, and after just a month and a half, the entire population has changed, by and large.

I'm part of a snapshot of life in here that will be out from under me before I know it.

There are some advantages to that. Less than two months isn't enough time for people to really get their clout set in stone and well known.

Sure, there are gangs. About a tenth of the inmates are gang members, most of them divided along ethnic lines. There are black, white, and Hispanic gangs, and then there are the skinheads, who even the other white gangs won't touch. Most everyone is a repeat offender. The stories are usually similar. They got caught up in all this when they were teenagers, and prison pipeline just does its dark magic to keep them behind bars.

The Russians weren't a gang before I got here, but now that I'm here and in charge, it's starting to look a lot like one. If that's the way the men want it, though, we're not going to act like a gang. We are the *bratva*. We have standards.

Each time I finish a rep on the bar, I catch a glimpse of the various people in the rec yard, some watching us, most minding their business. A couple of the skinheads are sporting black eyes thanks to me and my men.

We got a decent bit of information from them about the state of things in here over a few days. I've been here a short time, but I already know who the rats are, which guards are sympathetic to the skinheads, which are on the take from some of the gangs on the outside, and more importantly, how to safely keep in contact with the outside.

From there, it's just been a matter of staying in touch with my people to keep things running smoothly.

Between that and making one of the skinheads' toughest young fighters look like an angry brat on my first week here, I've made some waves in this detention center, for better or worse. Nobody has tried to come after us, but everyone's watching for their chance. It feels like being on the outside again.

This Nicole Burns, she intrigues me. I find myself thinking back to our meeting over and over again, thinking over each word that came from those pretty lips. Getting a second meeting is on my to-do list, but I have a feeling I am going to have trouble getting a leash on this one, much less keeping it there. She's wily and not to be underestimated. That's a mistake I made, and it's one I am sure my comrades will make without me out there guiding them.

I also know desire when I see it. It is written all over her face, in her eyes like a mirror looking back at me. She wants me, but I don't think for a second that she is naive enough to let that get the better of her.

And given her... personal problems, it may be harder to pin her down again.

Time will tell whether or not she sees reason and decides to do the right thing at my hearing.

A lot is riding on that hearing. More than I would like. If I don't end up at Ely State Prison, then I will be transferred to a federal prison out of state. That will make things a lot harder to run from inside, but I don't plan on losing Vegas so easily. Besides, in a federal prison, I'll be able to pull strings and set up alliances that I could not do even from the outside.

As I finish my reps, I see one of the other Russians making his way toward me. I get down from the bar and shake my arms out as I nod to him.

"Comrade," I say simply.

"I have a lead on getting word out to your estate, sir," he says, standing close enough to me that we won't be overheard. "If all goes well, we can get a request for bail to your subordinates within a week or so, as you requested."

"Good," I say, clapping him on the arm. "Keep me updated. Your service will be rewarded."

"Thank you, sir," he says with a respectful nod. The guards are eyeing us from across the yard. I only make brief eye contact with them, but enough to let them know I do not fear them.

Get bail, get out, and tie up loose ends. Those are my immediate goals. My assets have been frozen, though, and I can't access a penny of my own money. I have to rely on those under me, and if there is a chance someone is planning to move against me, that is not a good position to be in.

If I were an ambitious young man trying to climb the ranks swiftly, this would be the time I would strike, while the *pakhan* is behind bars and working through darker shadows than ever.

I watch the other men train for some time, guiding them and keeping them focused. Playing personal trainer for each other is how we bond when we are not watching our backs or focusing on business. It builds loyalty in a way only a prison can foster.

Exercise time ends at the usual time, and we start filing back indoors to get to our cells. Once I'm inside mine and settled, a guard approaches my cell door holding a stack of envelopes.

"Chaykovsky," the guard grunts, and he slips some mail into my cell. I raise my eyebrows. I was not expecting anything so soon, but without acknowledging the guard, I pick up the envelope and turn it over.

It has obviously been opened. All mail that comes to prisoners gets read and examined for suspicious content by censors, and it is very common for mail or items to get confiscated without notice to either the sender or the prisoner.

And indeed, the envelope is much bigger than necessary for how few items are in it, which tells me some things have been removed. It is addressed from Moscow. I find a few letters inside first, written in Russian, and at a glance, they look like simple personal letters from a family friend. I also find photographs—not actual photographs, since those are not allowed, but scanned and printed copies of real images.

The photos are of landscapes. There is a mountain in one, a quiet village in another, and a fox laying in the forest in the third.

This is code.

Reading over the letters themselves confirms this. The first of them is simple and short:

Dearest brother,

The mountain that we hiked for my fortieth birthday still stands strong, and the river that runs from it runs faster and colder than ever. I went there again with our cousins and found the same coins that we left in offering near the top. It is beautiful, and the hike went well. Our cousin's sister stayed behind to camp longer, and she loves the outdoors. We find rabbits that run fast in the burrows under the mountain. No fox can catch them. We love you very much and hope that the ground will not freeze this winter.

The other letters are much like it, just short and nonsensical personal letters that would never catch the attention of some underpaid censor among the guards. I doubt they even have someone who speaks Russian on their team, and if they do, glancing over this message wouldn't get attention.

I read over the others carefully, my eyes flitting over to the pictures with each line. Everything corresponds perfectly. The art of getting messages through prison censors is one we Russians know all too well.

By the end of the message, my eyebrows are raised. I cannot show too much emotion, or I might attract unwanted attention.

I fold the letters up and put them back into the envelope.

This is all a very interesting set of developments.

Time for dinner rolls around, and before we even get in line, I catch up with one of my most trusted associates and pull him aside.

"We need to discuss some news I've received," I say. "Some strings need to be pulled. *Now.*"

$\mathcal{I}$ have never hated a city more than I currently hate San Francisco. I am starting to really regret flying out here. Two days ago, when I first found out that my sister is missing and has been kidnapped for some kind of ransom, my initial impulse was to go straight back to the jail and demand to see Misha Chaykovsky again. That faint lilt of a Russian accent in the voice of my sister's kidnapper on the phone was the hint I needed to push me in that direction.

I swiveled around in the middle of the road and drove back several miles before it occurred to me how fruitless a conversation with Misha would be.

I have nothing to offer him in exchange for his help. It is because of me that the man is sitting behind bars right now. I am the one who brought him down and ruined his life.

The evidence is building against him, and there doesn't seem to be much hope for him at the moment. I know, deep down, I should feel happy about this. I gave solid evidence. I performed well under pressure. I survived and thrived in my undercover assignment and put a Russian mafia kingpin into custody. Those are all laudable feats, to be sure.

But instead of reveling in a job well done and raking in the kudos, my life has only been steadily unraveling ever since I first arrested Misha. First, my boss basically ripped me a new one for doing my damn job, propositioned me like the slimy jerk he is, and threatened my career.

Then, I got that fateful phone call from the San Francisco police department informing that my beloved baby sister is gone without a trace.

And that call from the kidnappers still echoes around in my head, the entire conversation replaying over and over like a broken record. The calm, calculating tone of his voice. The faint chatter in the background of a voice I could almost recognize. It feels like the answer is in my head somewhere, batted around between the stress and panic. I can't clear my head. Not even a brisk morning jog around the neighborhood where my hotel is located could shake these dark thoughts away.

All I can think about is Samantha… and Misha.

After I decided that talking to Misha would not do me any favors and would possibly count as a conflict of interest, I went ahead with my original gut-instinct plan: to fly out to San Francisco and do some investigating of my own.

I haven't taken a sick day or vacation day in years, so I have a little time saved up. Without much explanation, I called the secretary desk at Las Vegas Vice and informed him that I will be taking some time off. Personal time.

He asked for more information and pressed me to stay, since my case involving Misha and the Russian mafia is currently underway and they need all hands on deck. Especially me, since I am the one who arrested him and gathered the most intel. As much as it pained me to tell him no, to walk away from the case that could be the one to make or break my career in the force, I had to do it. I told him I was leaving and hung up the phone.

Ten minutes later, I boarded a last-minute flight to San Francisco, without even packing a bag first.

I knew that if I had gone home first to pack and prepare for the trip, I might lose my nerve and cave in. Besides, I am the kind of woman who prepares for anything and everything, so I keep a go-bag in the trunk of my car, complete with tiny toiletries and a few changes of clothes. So I eliminated any opportunity to rethink my plan.

I drove straight to the airport. I got on the plane and spent the whole flight nervously staring down at a crumpled photo of Sam and me as little kids. It has faded over time, but it's still easy to see the two of us grinning in our bathing suits, both holding our noses, wearing swim goggles. I can remember that day like it happened yesterday. We were at a resort in the Nevada desert meant to resemble an oasis paradise, complete with a water park. My sister and I were about to jump into a pool without floaties on our arms, the pay-off after a summer of swimming lessons at the community pool in our hometown. The photo captures us in a state of pure innocence, joy, and excitement. Jumping into the deep end of a pool, hand in hand, finally unafraid to swim freely.

It's a photo I've always kept in my wallet, a memory I treasure dearly. As a police officer, I know how dangerous it can be to keep personal items like that so close by. If a criminal were to snatch my wallet, they could find out a lot of information about me, including my weakness: Samantha. In fact, it seems like that is exactly what these kidnappers have done. They have stolen away the one truly bright spot in my life, the only person alive who still genuinely cares about me. And now I can't seem to track down any clue that might lead me to her.

From the moment I landed in California, I have been on the move. The past two nights I have barely slept, staying up late making clue boards, which in the light of morning just look like the ravings of a lunatic. I have been poring over old memories, checking her social media accounts obsessively, trying to dig up any clue as to where she might have last been seen.

Of course, I have not notified the San Fran police department that I'm here. I don't need them telling me to back off and let them handle it. It's just better if they don't know.

Besides, I'm not here so much as a cop as a concerned relative. I just happen to be a concerned relative with police training who is pretty damn good at tracking down people who don't want to be found. At vice, I've spent a lot of time tracking down fugitive drug lords and following breadcrumb trails to uncover the fraudulent accounts and offshore hoards that gamblers keep on retainer. I'm a damn bloodhound when I have a scent to follow.

Only this time, when it matters most, I keep coming up empty.

All day I have been running around town, chasing down leads that glimmer like a mirage of hope in the distance, only to dissipate into nothing when I get close enough to look. It's infuriating. Maddening. All the clues should be here, some-where, in this godforsaken beautiful town. I thought when I sent Samantha off to university here, she would be much safer than she could have been in Vegas. I know Vegas. I know its dark secrets, its dangerous underbelly, its ugly truths. And that is partly why I was so relieved when Sam told me she wanted to attend college in California. I thought to myself, *well, this will be a good fit for her. She'll be away from the neon lights and fast living of Las Vegas.*

But I guess I was wrong. One thing I am learning as a police officer and as an adult navigating this harsh world is that there is no real safe place. There is no city on the planet where one can be totally free from fear. I used to think becoming a cop would make me feel fearless and powerful, but instead, I just feel small. And never more than right now, chasing after ghosts.

Last night I spent hours and hours tracking down the full name and contact information for Sam's college roommate. I know their address, roughly, but I wanted to know more about the girl my sister has been living with for months. I scoured Samantha's Facebook account, looking through every single photo uploaded, every comment posted, every status update for the past six months. Finally, I managed to find a photo she uploaded a month ago with a caption that reads: BEST ROOMIE EVER!!!

It's a picture of my sister with her chin-length dark hair and brown eyes standing with her arm around another girl, who is taller, blonde, and equally pretty. My heart raced at the sight of those two smiling young women, and my hands were shaking as I hovered the cursor over the blonde girl's face. To my relief, a name popped up. She is tagged in the photo.

The name: Alyssa Folger.

So, naturally, I spent the rest of the night scouring Alyssa's social media accounts, looking for an email address or a phone number. Sure, I could have just messaged her via Facebook, but I wanted a more direct link to her. Finally, after hours of looking around the Internet, I settled for her school email address. I sent her a message, asking if we could meet up to talk about Sam.

And thank god for how tech-obsessed the kids are these days, because she answered me within hours with the promise of meeting for a coffee on campus in the morning. I fell asleep at my laptop right after receiving the message, but still managed to wake up on time to drag my exhausted body out of the hotel and down to the campus.

I've been sitting in this crowded cafe overrun with nervous freshmen carrying huge stacks of books, looking terrified, for hours. I keep checking the time on my cell phone, waiting for Alyssa to show up. I might be a little early — by an hour — but still. I don't have time to wait on her. My sister is out there somewhere, in trouble. Possibly hurt. Or worse.

Just when I'm about to give up and walk out, a tall, pretty blonde girl comes into the cafe. She's looking around everywhere, squinting like she's searching for someone. That has to be her. I stand up and gesture for her to walk over. She gives me a nervous smile and comes to sit down across from me.

"Hi, are you Alyssa Folger?" I ask, holding out my hand for her to shake.

"Yeah. I'm Sam's roommate. You her sister?" she says, shaking my hand.

"Yes. I'm Nicole," I answer. "Do you want anything? Coffee? A muffin?"

She shrugs. "No, thank you. I'm okay. I actually don't have much time. I have a class starting in twenty minutes," Alyssa admits, looking apologetic.

"Oh. That's okay. That's fine. It shouldn't take too long. I just have some questions about where you think she might have disappeared to," I explain, lowering my voice. "When was the last time you saw Sam?"

Alyssa bites her lip, thinking it over. "Oh, probably four days ago, I think?"

"Four days," I repeat under my breath, my heart racing. "So she'd already been missing for two days when the police filed a missing person's report?"

"I guess so," Alyssa answers. She looks nervous, like she's in trouble or something. It dawns on me that Samantha probably told her that I'm a police officer, so I might be a little bit intimidating to her.

"Hey, listen. You're not in trouble," I assure her, forcing a sympathetic smile. "I'm not mad at you and I don't blame you for anything. I just wanted to talk to you because you seem like someone who was — is — close to my sister. Were you good friends?"

"Yeah," she says, nodding. "Sam is an awesome friend, great roommate. She always does her dishes and mine, even if I don't ask her to. She knows I hate doing the dishes, but I don't mind doing laundry, so we split those chores." A faint smile crosses her face, and I can tell that Samantha's disappearance has done a number on her, too. I feel a twinge of kinship with this almost complete stranger, bonding over how amazing Sam is. She's always been the most patient, kind, and thoughtful person I know.

"Sounds like a good system," I say, folding my hands in front of me on the table. "So, what do you think happened? Did you guys have a fight or something? The police here seem to think she's a runaway. But that just doesn't seem like the Sam I know."

"No, we've never had a fight, actually. I've never had a roommate I get along with so well before. In freshman year, I had to room with this girl who would leave her dirty clothes all over the bathroom floor. It was gross," Alyssa says, wrinkling her nose.

"Sounds awful," I agree, although at the moment I honestly could not care less. "So in the days leading up to her disappearance, was she acting funny?"

"Funny?" Alyssa asks, tilting her head to one side.

"Like, was she more moody than usual? Did she

seem depressed or anxious? More quiet than usual?" I pressed her.

Alyssa shook her head vigorously. "God, no. If anything, she seemed happier than usual. I mean, she's always in a good mood, but she just seemed really excited about something."

"Like what?" I inquire, hoping this could lead somewhere.

"I don't know," she admits with a sigh. "I'm so sorry. I wish I could give you more information, but I just wasn't paying that much attention. I have exams coming up, so I've been studying pretty much nonstop."

"It's okay," I tell her, leaning back in the chair. "It's not your fault."

"I really miss her already," Alyssa confesses. "The apartment feels so empty and quiet without Sam. I hope she comes back soon."

"Me, too," I sigh. I glance down at the time on my cell phone. "Well, it looks like you need to be getting to class soon. Sorry to interrupt your morning."

"It's no problem. It was really nice to meet you, though I wish it were under better circumstances. You know, Sam talked about you all the time. She really loved you a lot," she says, standing up and pushing in her chair.

I can feel the tears stinging in my eyes. I wish people would stop referring to Sam in the past tense.

She's still alive. It's only been four days. There is still hope.

"Thank you, Alyssa. Good to meet you, too. If you think of anything else—"

"I'll message you," she answers with a quick smile. "Bye."

"Bye," I reply, waving as she rushes out the door. I stare down at the espresso in front of me, wondering what the hell else I'm supposed to do now. I've already called the police department from a pay phone to ask for more information, so they wouldn't know it's me. I've walked all over campus, looking for clues, asking random strangers if they know Sam. I've done an in-depth tour of her neighborhood. And now I've interviewed her roommate.

I'm at a complete loss. I have run all over this town looking for any sign of my sister. I don't know what I expected to find when I flew out here, but with every moment that passes, it feels like she's only getting farther and farther away.

My street smarts, my police training, none of it has led me anywhere useful. I know I still have one lead left untapped back in Nevada, but I am loathe to use it.

Misha.

He's the only one left I have not interrogated. It feels like a long shot, but at this point, I am starting to wonder if he's all I've got. My only hope lies in a soon-to-be convicted criminal. A criminal *I* helped arrest. And he's still there, waiting around, wasting precious hours behind bars.

He's a captive audience.

I could go back and interrogate him until he cracks. I have the upper hand here, don't I? I could rattle his cage, stir up some new information that might just point me in a more helpful direction. But after the shitshow our last meeting was, I don't think I can face him. I may have the upper hand legally, but he's got something over me, too.

My attraction to him. It's undeniable. Obvious. And he knows it. If I want to keep my job and maintain my sanity, I need to stay away from him. Even if he is my last hope.

My phone rings and I quickly answer it before the ringtone can disturb my fellow cafe patrons too much. "Hello?" I answer quietly.

"Hi, this is Dave. From vice? Your cubicle is catty-corner to mine."

I frown in confusion. "Okay. Dave. What is it? If Harden is trying to get me to come back right now, you can just tell him to shove it up—"

"No, no. I'm just calling to tell you that the evidence against, uh, My-shuh Chay… Chay… Kov…"

"Misha Chaykovsky, yes, what about him?" I interrupt impatiently.

"Yeah, him. Uh, the evidence for his case has gone missing."

"What?" I cry out, slamming my hands on the table as I stand up in shock. Annoyed cafe-goers glare over at me and I sit back down, lowering my voice. "What?"

"Mhmm. A good bit of it is gone. So, looks like they're going to have to release the guy by three PM on Friday unless you come back to testify."

"Shit," I swear, leaning my face into my palm. "Okay. Okay. Just… hold down the fort until I get there, alright?"

"Whatever you say, Officer."

I hang up and let out a groan of frustration. I don't have time for this.

Just as I'm about to chug my coffee down and get another one, my phone lights up with a text message. I open it, annoyed, thinking it's another message from the Las Vegas PD. But when I read the message, my heart sinks.

"Oh no," I murmur, getting up so quickly I knock over my coffee. Not even bothering to clean it up, I run out of the cafe and jump into my rental car.

I have to get back to Nevada. Now.

"Are both parties ready to proceed?"

My gaze at the court clerk is even and steady. My orange prisoner's uniform is in stark contrast to the crisp, starchy suits of the lawyers and officials all around me, but I hold my head high with dignity. I will not be made a mockery of, not even at my own hearing.

"Yes, your honor," says the attorney to my right. Seated next to her is Nicole, looking professional and composed as ever. She didn't make eye contact with me when we entered the courtroom, but her face is resolute. I know the look. She means to put me away today.

"Yes, your honor," my attorney echoes. My lawyer is an older woman with a face like a hawk's and eyes twice as ravenous. She's one of the best in the state. If there's anyone who could hold a candle to a sting operation like this, it's her.

The clerk gives a quick nod and sweeps out of the room, leaving us in uncomfortable silence for a few moments. I'm still as a statue. A moment later, the clerk reappears at the door, and behind him, the judge enters, a tall and broad-shouldered man with more wrinkles on his forehead than I could count.

"All rise. Court is now in session with the Honorable Judge McKenzie presiding."

The judge takes a seat and waves his hand at everyone in the room who stands. It's a quick, routine entry, and I can tell this is an experienced man.

"You may be seated," he says in a weary voice, and we sit. As soon as we are seated, he reviews a few papers in front of him before leaning forward into his microphone and pronouncing in a slow, deliberate tone, "I'd like to call the case of *The People of Las Vegas v. Misha Chaykovsky*, case number 5M55434. The hearing will proceed as follows: Each party will present a brief opening statement telling the court what they intend to prove and why they intend to prove the issue that is to be decided."

His gravelly tone is rehearsed and practiced, but I feel electricity in the air around me nonetheless.

"After opening statements, the parties will present their evidence. The plaintiff will go first in both cases," he adds with a nod to the table where

Nicole and her lawyer are seated. "They will testify, thoroughly, and call any necessary witnesses and written evidence. As the plaintiff testifies, the defense will have the chance to examine or reexamine statements the witness gives. Afterward, the same courtesy will be given to the defense, who may call witnesses and present evidence in turn."

Some of my associates are present in court, and my attorney was able to put together a reasonable defense from the handful of my associates who she determined would be able to come forward and present something tangible. But it's their word against an undercover police officer's, which the judge will favor.

In short, the situation does not look good.

The judge rattles off the remainder of the formalities, then opens the floor for the plaintiff's attorney to make his opening statement. The young lawyer stands up next to Nicole, and I see her eyes watching him carefully. There is something in her expression that seems off, but I can't put my finger on it.

"Thank you, your honor," the attorney said. "My client and I are here to bring justice to Misha Chaykovsky, the alleged de facto leader of an elaborate and organized Russian crime syndicate in the city of Las Vegas, informally known as the *bratva*."

I have to hold back a smile. It sounds dramatic when he puts it like that. I should have lawyers introduce me more often.

"We believe Mr. Chaykovsky to have carried out a number of illegal operations for profit in the city and throughout the state of Nevada, both by proxy and in person. The arresting officer, Nicole Burns, conducted an undercover operation for several months to gather the evidence that we intend to present today. The charges against Mr. Chaykovsky today include racketeering, drug trafficking, and tax evasion. Should the case against Mr. Chaykovsky be allowed to proceed, the LVPD has reason to believe the charges of murder in the first degree, grand larceny, arson, and carrying out a number of notorious and unsolved contract killings within the city."

I lean back in my chair, presenting myself as relaxed as possible. A lot of that statement was pure bravado. Nicole might get me on trafficking, but racketeering will be hard to prove, and all the rest is just smoke. But the opening statement is not yet finished.

"Officer Burns," he says with a gesture to her, "got acquainted closely with Mr. Chaykovsky in her time undercover and will act as the sole witness today. Mr. Chaykovsky has close ties to his associates in Moscow, and given his resources and connections, we believe he is a significant flight risk, and the prosecution requests no bail."

When the prosecuting attorney finished, my attorney stands up to present my opening statement, a much briefer rebuttal.

"Your honor," she starts, "my client is a successful businessman in Las Vegas and a boon to the local economy. He is a job creator and a shrewd negotiator, as the witnesses I have gathered will attest. The charges leveled at him by Officer Burns are founded on evidence that I will demonstrate is not admissible in court because of a number of procedural violations she committed on the job."

Nicole glances my way, and I know she's wondering if I told my attorney that we had sex. I crack her the faintest ghost of a smile just to make her nervous, and she looks away from me.

In truth, I didn't tell the attorney that. I am not completely sure why I didn't. Part of me thinks it would just be useless baggage to drag out that she could easily twist into a prostitution charge. I know that's not all of it, though.

Still, it's nice to see her squirm as payback for arresting me.

My attorney names a few other technicalities that would hopefully throw out the case, but I know that I had been caught red-handed. All Nicole has to do is tell them how things went down, and it would be all the judge needed to hear.

They were right to consider me a flight risk, because I'd be on a plane to Moscow first thing in the morning if I was granted bail.

A few minutes and formalities later, Nicole is walking up to the witness stand. We lock eyes for a few moments as she went, and those eyes of hers were unreadable.

It is such a strange, stark difference from the gleaming eyes I saw when my cock entered her in my penthouse. She was able to bring up so much desire and promise in a single glance, but now, she is able to keep her true intentions completely masked.

She is a damn fine actress, or a very complicated person, and I'm starting to think she may be a little of both. I couldn't have asked for a more worthy enemy, at least.

"State your full name for the court, please," the judge asks her once she is on the stand.

"Nicole Burns," she replies.

"Do you swear that the evidence you are about to give is the truth, the whole truth, and nothing but the truth, so help you god?"

"Yes," she answers, never breaking eye contact with the judge.

"Officer Burns," the judge begins in a less formal voice as he reviews some papers in front of him, "your attorney says you were the arresting officer at Mr. Chaykovsky's establishment. Is that correct?"

"Yes, your honor," she says. There's such a tense silence in the court under her words that we could have heard a pin drop.

"Please explain the nature of your undercover work."

"I spent three months working as a dancer at

various clubs on the Strip under the stage name Misty," she says. "In that time, I got to know a number of Mr. Chaykovsky's associates, as well as him himself, briefly. My purpose was to get evidence to convict him on the suspicion that he orchestrated and carried out the crimes he's being charged with. I arrested him just before a police search of the establishment when I believed I had enough evidence to bring to the court."

"And what evidence did you find?" the judge asks.

Nicole's eyes want to go to me. I notice the faintest twitch of her face. The silence is so thick I could cut it with a finger before the next words come out of her mouth.

"We found nothing, your honor."

The words dropped like an anvil in the court. Nicole's attorney's face goes white. My attorney's jaw drops. There's a murmuring among the crowd, and the people start whispering to each other in agitation.

I'm as still as a statue, but I'm more shocked than anyone else in the room.

"Your statement appears to be controversial, Officer Burns," the judge says, leaning forward. "Do you care to explain yourself?"

"The search of Mr. Chaykovsky's establishment turned up no evidence against him," she repeats. Her expression is completely blank.

She's lying under oath, and she's the only one who can get away with it.

"Officer Burns," her attorney says, standing up quickly, "I should remind you that you have a number of items on the police's inventory from the investigation-"

"These items do not exist," she says firmly, "and you will not find them at the police station. This was a mistake on my part, and I accept responsibility for it."

My attorney looks to me with an alarmed yet meaningful expression. She's worked with mobsters before. She can tell when a witness has been blackmailed.

I simply look back at her with mild surprise, as if this is all just a convenient coincidence. I'm as good at hiding my emotions as Nicole is, and now is more important than ever for that.

"Just to be perfectly clear," the judge says with an annoyed sigh, "are you, Nicole Burns, saying under oath that you no longer have evidence to present in the case against Misha Chaykovsky, as you came to this hearing to present?"

"That is what I am saying, your honor," she affirms. Her attorney runs his hands through his hair and flips his folder closed, sitting back down, defeated.

"Is there a reason I should not hold you in

contempt of court for wasting our time, Officer Burns?" the judge asks sternly.

"This is new information to me," she says, "and that is all I can say at this time."

The judge looks to the prosecuting attorney, who simply gives a resigned shrug back, and the judge nods.

"Very well. Misha Chaykovsky, with the apparent lack of evidence, I have no choice but to hereby clear you of all charges. You will be processed and released in twenty-four hours. The city of Las Vegas apologizes for this miscarriage of justice."

The judge's gavel bangs, and just like that, I am a free man.

I allow myself a smile, and I shake hands with my attorney, whose look of relief tells me just how close we came to disaster.

I stand up as the bailiff comes to escort me back to transportation to the detention center, but before I walk out of the courtroom, I look over to Nicole.

If looks could kill…

The anger in her eyes is venomous. Off the stand, she doesn't need to hold anything back. She and everyone else in the courtroom knows what just happened, but nobody feels it as sharply as Nicole. She doesn't have to make any signals at me to get her message across.

She wants her sister freed, and she wants it to happen now.

I give her a wink in reply.

That only twists the dagger, but the way I see it, we're even now, the two of us. If Nicole thinks I'm a man who can be taken so easily, she's mistaken.

I march back to the van that will take me back to the detention center, but that look I saw on Nicole's face stays with me. I know this won't be the last I see of her, and I have a feeling our meeting is going to happen sooner rather than later.

But for now, I can enjoy the taste of freedom finally within my grasp. I have just twenty-four hours to settle my affairs in the detention center. And of course, I do not plan to forget my allies who helped me behind bars. I'll pull all the strings I have to in order to make it know that their service is appreciated.

Misha Chaykovsky rewards his loyal soldiers.

And in the coming days, I have a feeling that I'm going to need each and every loyal soul. I may have avoided prison and survived everything it can throw at me, but I still have the threats from the outside to worry about.

It's a long road ahead of me.

And if Nicole wants to be a player in it all so badly, I am going to make that happen.

This time, it will be on my terms.

If someone had told me a week ago that I would be committing career suicide yesterday, I would have laughed in their face. Maybe even slapped them across the face. Being a cop has been my dream ever since I was a little girl, idolizing my father in his uniform, shaking hands with people, breaking up fights, settling disputes, keeping our little hometown safe from the big, scary world outside.

A week ago, I would have told you that nothing, and I mean nothing, could ever come between me and my dreams.

But that was before my sister went missing. That was before I met a man named Misha Chaykovsky, the Russian gangster who has been transformed in my mind from a high-stakes criminal to the only man in the world who might be able to help me find my sister.

Screw my undercover mission at the strip club; this, right here, right now, is my most important case ever.

And that is why, on this gloriously sunny Saturday morning, I am pacing back and forth in the waiting room of the detention center, listening to the clank of metal bars, the shouting and swearing of inmates. I can smell the musty scent of unwashed male bodies, men bustling around, shoving each other, building alliances and breaking trusts.

It's a damn jungle in there, and I'm hanging around just several yards away, behind the security line, safe but still too close for comfort. Truth be told, I really hate visiting jails and prisons. That should go without saying, but in the police department, I have several colleagues who have admitted they kind of look forward to it. They like getting to come here and see the fruits of their labor, the 'bad guys' behind bars while the 'good guys' walk free.

But it doesn't feel like that to me, not really. All I feel is awkward and uncomfortable. Totally out of place. And I look around at the faces of the men in here and some of them look too familiar. I'm reminded that they're all just people, living out the consequences of, in a lot of cases, merely bad judgement.

Well, that, and the fact that I get whistled at and

jeered at every time I come here. Because I am one of the very few women who ever passes through these doors, and the touch-starved men in here will take whatever they can get, even if it's just a modestly-dressed cop with her hair in a messy ponytail and not a stitch of makeup on her face.

Today, I don't care all too much about appearances.

In fact, I don't really care at all.

I have been way too distracted by the mystery surrounding Sam's disappearance to take much time for a shower. I'm clean, but I haven't ironed my clothes or put much thought into an outfit. Yesterday, in court, was the first time I've worn a nice outfit in days. And that was purely because it's court, and I am in fact still a police officer, so I have to dress for the occasion.

Even if I was destroying my career.

But today? I'm just wearing a random wrinkled blouse from the pile on my chair in my bedroom paired with a pencil skirt that might just be a little too short after it shrunk in the wash slightly. I pulled on a pair of nylons and some black heels to finish the outfit, then ran out of the house and rushed all the way here to the jail for my date with the prisoner.

I am here to collect Misha Chaykovsky. He is being released very soon, any minute, in fact. And I expect to be the first person he sees. He may have lucked out of his sentence for now, but I am not about to let him squirm away from me yet, not when he might just be the only chance I have at finding Samantha.

He's coming with me, whether he likes it or not. Of course, things here at the detention center move about as quickly as molasses, so I'm getting a little impatient. I have been here for over an hour, waiting for the guards to bring Misha out so I can snatch him.

I storm over to the front desk, which is sheltered by a thick pane of impenetrable Plexiglas, and knock on the little window. The crotchety older woman at the computer looks up at me through horn-rimmed glasses with a sour look on her face. Reluctantly, she slides the window open.

"Yes?" she grunts grumpily.

"Sorry, but how much longer is this going to take?" I ask, leaning on the counter with one elbow while I squint down the hall. She heaves a dramatic sigh.

"I don't know how to answer that question. I'm just the front desk secretary, ma'am," she replies, shrugging. I fix her with a solemn glare.

"It's Officer, not ma'am," I correct quickly. "Look, I'm on kind of a tight schedule here. Is there any way we could, I don't know, expedite this process a little bit?"

She blinks slowly at me.

"Expedite the process of releasing a high-risk criminal from a state detention center, you mean?" she says pointedly.

I pinch the bridge of my nose, trying desperately to stay calm.

"Yes. Okay. I see your point. This kind of thing can't be rushed. I understand. It's just that—"

"Oh, here they come," she interrupts, jerking a thumb back down the hall.

"Really?" I pipe up, my heart racing as I jump away to look down the hallway. As soon as I'm away from the counter, the front desk lady slams the window shut and turns away. I look over, stunned into silence. There's no one coming down the hall.

"She tricked me," I murmur in awe. "Wow."

For half a second I consider banging on the window to yell at her, but I think better of it. After all, that woman has no control over what goes on inside the jail. It's not like she can speed things along any better than I could. So I force myself to go take a seat, but I can't tear my eyes away from the hallway. I can still hear the jeers and shouts of inmates inside, and I can't help but wonder if any of the voices I'm hearing belong to Misha.

It's another good thirty minutes or so before the door opens and three figures come striding up the hallway. I jump to my feet, my stomach twisting into knots. Is it him?

I rush over to see that is, in fact, two of the

biggest, burliest guards the jail has to offer, leading Misha Chaykovsky out toward the waiting room. Finally.

Seeing Misha's face makes my heart skip a beat, which is very annoying, considering how angry I am with him. I'm downright pissed off. But his face lights up at the sight of me, which makes butterflies flit around in my stomach.

Get a grip, I warn myself. *You're Officer Nicole Burns, not Misty. Not anymore.*

"Officer Burns," greets the same guard who helped me days ago when I came to interview Misha. "What are you doing here? How's it going?"

"Oh, it's good. I'm good. How are you?" I ask awkwardly, dragging my eyes away from Misha to give the guard a polite smile.

"Can't complain," he replies jovially. "You here to pick up this fellow?"

"Yes, sir," I answer tersely, looking back at Misha. The Mafioso looks rather amused to see me, like I'm the last person he expected to meet out here on release day. But I know that's definitely just a cover. He knows exactly why I'm here, even if he's trying to play coy right now.

"Well, Mr. Chaykovsky, it's been a real pleasure. Hope you enjoyed your stay at Club Med. Come back and see us soon," jokes the guard. Misha and I both look at him quizzically.

He shrugs and chuckles. "Just a little jailhouse humor. Anyways, have a good one."

He heads back down the hallway, leaving the other guard to roll his eyes and shake his head, sighing. The guard gets out a key and frees Misha's wrists and ankles, watching him carefully as though the Mafioso might suddenly start swinging punches or something. But Misha just stands there stoically, staring at me with those piercing blue eyes. Something about his unbroken gaze makes me feel so vulnerable. Exposed. Like he can cut right through the bullshit and see the truth underneath it all. Like he can peer right into my soul.

I swallow hard, hoping he can't hear my heart pounding away in my chest.

"Come with me," I tell him, snapping my fingers. He raises one heavy dark brow at the gesture, but I can't tell if he's amused, offended, or possibly both.

"Let us know if he gives you any trouble," says the guard, watching Misha with suspicious eyes. "Have a good day, Miss."

"It's Officer," I correct him, but give him a patient smile anyway. "And same to you."

Then I turn back to Misha and start marching out of the jail with the Mafioso trailing after me, striding along at a slow, casual pace. It really seems like nothing ruffles his feathers. He's cool and calm no matter what.

It's infuriating.

As soon as we get out to the parking lot, I whip around and glare at him, gritting my teeth.

"What?" he asks, shrugging.

"Oh, like you don't know," I sneer. "Come on. Get in the car."

I point to my little red hatchback and a flicker of amusement plays across his features. "You want me to get into that car," he says, deadpan.

"Yes. Obviously," I sigh, tapping my foot.

"In the passenger seat. Of a cherry-red hatch-back," Misha continues.

"Yes! Get in. Now," I urge him, giving his arm a light nudge.

"I don't have to do anything you say, you know," he tells me.

I roll my eyes.

"Right. So, what's your plan then? To walk home? Where even is your home? Where are you really from?"

Misha smirks, that familiar old flame blazing behind his eyes.

"If I remember correctly, you know where I live. You've been there."

My cheeks start to burn and I smack him on the arm.

"Get in the car!" I shout.

Finally, he relents and gets gingerly into the passenger seat of my car. If I wasn't so pissed off, I might have laughed. My car is the perfect size for me, but Misha has got to be well over six-foot-five and bulging with muscles. He's folded up in the passenger seat like an accordion. He looks like he's in a child's Barbie car or something.

Serves him right. Maybe he'll be a little less intimidating like this.

"Where are we headed, captain?" he asks, giving me a sidelong glance.

I start up the engine and start to pull away from the detention center. I keep my eyes on the road, refusing to look at him.

"Come on. Don't play dumb with me," I mutter.

"Wouldn't dream of it," Misha says, rather cryptically. "But really, where are we going?"

I glance over at him, frowning.

"You can drop that act now. We're not at the jail anymore. It's just you and me. Cut to the damn chase, Chaykovsky."

"Oh, so we're back on last-name terms now?" he quips. "I would think by now we'd at least be upgraded to first names. Nicole."

"Let's get one thing straight right off the bat," I tell him firmly. "It was Misty you slept with, not Nicole. And that's way behind us now. That was a mistake."

"Well, tell Misty I had a damn good time," he replies coyly.

I very nearly slam on the brakes, I'm so angry, but I force myself to calm down. I have to remain composed in this situation. My sister's life is on the line. We ride in silence for a few minutes, then Misha reaches over to lay a huge hand on my arm.

"What are you doing?" I ask, annoyed. I jerk my arm away.

He looks almost hurt.

"I was going to thank you. For getting me out of there."

"Whatever. I didn't do it for you," I retort.

"Either way, you did me a huge favor by destroying that evidence," he continues. "I will never be able to properly repay you for that."

I'm so stunned that I have to swerve to avoid a massive crack in the road.

"Excuse me? You think *I* had anything to do with that?" I shout.

"Well, if not you, then who else?" he asks.

"You did! You and your mafia cronies or whatever! Stop messing around," I reply.

"I'm serious," Misha says grimly. "I had nothing to do with that. And I thought... since you lied under oath for me..."

"Shh! Jesus, keep your voice down," I shoot back instinctively.

"Why? We're the only ones here. Unless you have reason to believe your tiny little car has been bugged or something," he jokes.

"Stop. Stop lying. I know you're behind all this," I accuse. "I know you somehow got that evidence taken care of and I know you're the one behind what happened to my sister."

He's silent for a moment, taking it all in. Like he's shocked. Then he says softly, "That's what you were on the phone about that day."

"Yes, asshole. Someone took her and they're holding her for ransom. Yeah. They already called and told me all about it, so you can drop the ignorance game. I know you're in on this. Hell, you probably orchestrated the whole damn thing just to get back at me for putting you in jail. Well, you're out now, and you're going to help me set this shit straight," I demand.

"You really think I planned this?" Misha asks slowly.

"Of course. Who the hell else would do this? I'm just a low-ranking vice cop. Nobody cares about me. Nobody targets me. No one worth their salt has any reason to hold a grudge against me. Except for you," I explain.

"Nicole," he says solemnly. "I am not lying to you. I don't have anything to do with what happened to your sister. I didn't get rid of the evidence. I don't know how this happened. I thought you were the one who disposed of the evidence all this time. You lied in court to get me out, so it all made sense."

"I-I wouldn't," I stammer, suddenly feeling my entire plan unravel. "You didn't?"

"No. I didn't," he assures me.

"Then who the hell did it?" I murmur.

"Someone who wanted me out of jail," he reasons.

"And you and I... both of us..." I trail off.

"We were pawns in someone else's game," Misha says darkly.

"This is bigger than you and me, isn't it?" I ask softly.

I glance over to see Misha nodding. But just then, there's a squealing of tires somewhere behind us. I look in the rearview mirror to see a flashy black sports car trailing us. No, not just trailing us.

Chasing us.

"What the hell?" I mutter. The black car speeds up rapidly, its engine roaring.

"Time to see how fast this little toy car can go," Misha says quickly. "What are you waiting for? Hit the gas! Go, go go!"

I slam my foot down on the gas pedal, my little red car whirring madly as we speed off down the empty highway. Clouds of desert dust kick up in our wake, but I can still see the black car zooming through the puffs.

"Who the hell is that?" I exclaim, my heart racing.

"I don't know, but we absolutely cannot wait to find out," Misha growls. "Faster!"

"It's a four-cylinder, Misha, it's doing the best it can!" I shout back angrily.

"We have to lose him. He's gaining on us," he adds.

"Not helping!" I retort, throwing my car into a higher gear.

"Is there anywhere we can go?" he asks. "We have to shake him off."

"Oh, god. I don't know. Uh, let me think," I answer, wracking my brain. Then, it hits me. I know a place down a dirt road, a random turn off this highway. If I can get our stalker close enough, then take the turn fast enough, he might topple. My little car is so low to the ground and well-centered, I think I can swing it.

I don't have any other plan. This one will have to do.

We ride along at top speed for several more minutes, as I swerve and jerk the wheel intentionally to kick up more dust, trying to blind the guy following us. Finally, I see the turn coming up. Now or never.

"What's your plan?" Misha yells over the roar of the engine.

"Hold on!"

"What? That's not a—"

"I said *hold on!*"

I slow down just enough to force the guy behind us to slam on his brakes, and at the last second, I jerk the wheel all the way to the right, peeling out and nearly toppling my car over in the process as I turn down the dirt road toward the place I have not visited in years. This act kicks up so much sand and dust that at first we can't see anything behind us, but when it clears a little, we can see that our assailant's car has completely flipped over and is sliding down a dusty dune in a heap of screaming metal.

"Holy shit!" I cry out. "It worked! It fucking worked!"

"Amazingly, yes, it has," Misha agrees, clearly both concerned and impressed at the same time. I give him an exhilarated smile, before I remember that I'm supposed to be angry at him.

"Now, where are we going?" he asks one more time.

"To a place where nobody will come looking for us," I reply.

I step out of the car and look up at the building in front of us, and I furrow my eyebrows before a smile crosses my lips.

"I know this place," I say simply.

"I'm sure you do," she says back with irritation in her voice as she marches toward the doors. "Don't suppose you have your hands around this place too, do you?"

"No," I admit, admiring the large building as I follow her at a slower pace. "I have no ties to brothels, Officer."

She rolls her eyes at me and rings the doorbell as I approach.

"I must admit, I'm surprised to hear that you do, though," I add, quirking an eyebrow at her. She doesn't look at me, but she frowns, crossing her arm as she's waits for someone to answer.

I'm mostly surprised because this brothel is outside the Las Vegas metropolitan area, meaning it's outside her jurisdiction. She seems like she knows this place, but she can't have been working vice here.

The door finally opens, and the smell of perfume wafts out to overwhelm us both. A middle-aged woman with red hair steps out and recognizes Nicole immediately, her face brightening up and her arms spreading out.

"Oh my god, Nicole, good to see you! Come here, honey," she gushes, and Nicole meets her in a friendly hug.

"Hey, Krystal," Nicole replies. "Is Mama Daisy in?"

"Sure is," she says, holding the door open wider. "Come on in. Who's your friend?" She looks me up and down apprehensively, then glances between the two of us.

"A friend," she says curtly, and Krystal just raises her eyebrows, not looking like she wanted to pry further.

We don't have to look for the house manager very long. Within a few seconds, a tall woman in a fetching white coat appears around the corner of the hallway and seems as happy to see Nicole as Krystal was.

"Nicky, honey!" she says, stepping forward and

taking her hands, kissing her on each cheek. "Oh, here I thought I'd seen the last of you."

"I'm not that easy to shake," she says with a nervous laugh. "How is everything?"

"Honey, business is booming, but I won't bore you with the details. What brings you back around these parts?"

As I step in after Nicole and Krystal closes the door behind us, I get a better look at the place. It's classy, but not too over-the-top ritzy. I've never actually been inside. The walls are a dark purple, and the floors are black and shining. Dim red lights glow along the walls, and of course, it wouldn't be a brothel without erotic paintings lining every bit of free space on those purple walls. The occasional lavish red curtain hangs here and there for dramatic effect, and in the main lobby beyond us, I can see a big chandelier hanging from the ceiling.

"Kind of a long story," she admits, earning a sympathetic smile from the manager. "I'd love to catch up a little, but first, I was wondering if my friend and I could borrow a room for the night? I've got some cash on me, and-"

"Oh, go off with your cash!" Daisy says with a laugh, waving a hand. "Of course you can have a room, no charge. It's going to be a slow night tonight, it'll give the girls something to chat about," she adds with a knowing wink in my direction.

"Thanks," Nicole says warmly as Krystal hurries to get us a room key and tosses it to Nicole.

"Room 204," she says briskly. "Come find me when the two of you have had a chance to settle in, hm?"

"Of course, Madame," I say in a low rumble with a smile, and the manager giggles and winks at Nicole, who looks mortified.

"Come on," she grumbles at me, and I follow her up the stairs.

"So," I start once we're trudging up carpeted wooden stairs to the second floor. The scent of perfume only gets stronger the higher we get, and the colors on the walls and paintings seem to pop all the more. "How *does* a woman like you get so cozy with a place like this? Do they know…?"

"No," she says in a low but sharp voice, casting a glance over her shoulder. I meant to ask whether the brothel knows she's a cop, and she picked up on that. "I knew this place before I took my current job."

"My my," I say as we reach the second floor and head toward our room. "You become a more interesting woman each time we speak."

"Not like that," she groans, and she sticks the key into the keyhole to get the heavy door open. "My best friend in college, Trish, she started working here for a while. I hated the idea, so I followed her and rented a room for a week to keep an eye on things."

She cracks the door open, and the interior is everything you would expect. The bed is huge and covered in red sheets, the floors and walls are a richer hue of purple, and the bedframe is painted gold. There's a sink in the corner of the room, and the place smells like a mixture of an expensive perfume store and a dive bar.

I shut the door behind us, and the solid click tells me it's soundproof.

"Aw, you played babysitter?" I tease.

"Not exactly," she says gruffly. "As you can see, I... kind of fell in love with the place. The people here are nice," she admits with a smile as she crosses the room to the sink and splashes a little water in her face. "I decided that as long as my friend was being safe and sticking to the right people, I'd support her, and I ended up making a lot of friends here."

"That's very charitable of you, Officer Burns," I say with emphasis on the last bit, and she winces.

"Seriously, keep quiet about that here. Please?" she asks, and I chuckle.

"Don't want to lose your street cred, eh?"

"My friends and family are important to me."

My teasing smile grows more sincere, and I step closer to her, lowering my voice.

"I meant what I said, by the way. In the car. I had nothing to do with your sister being taken. I was informed about it, though, after it happened."

She furrows her eyebrows at me, and I take out

the envelope I received in jail and spread out the contents on top of the drawers.

"See here," I say, "these pictures line up to what's written in the letters. It's a coded message. I got it not long before the hearing. I assumed some of my men were taking initiative and acting without my orders. I never gave word to make this happen."

She examines the pictures, narrowing her eyes. "What does it say?"

"It says your little sister has been successfully taken, that she is safe and being treated well, and she is being held for ransom at a secure location. The kidnappers have already made contact with you, and gotten their message across. This is not a ransom for money. It is a ransom for a favor. I thought that favor was to release me. Now... I'm not so sure."

"That makes sense, but give me a reason to believe you."

I smile. She never loses her edge.

"Besides admitting weakness and having no reason to lie to you? If I had her taken, I'd have no reason to keep her in hiding after what you did for me. I'm a man who repays his debts." I smile wolfishly. "You lied on the stand for me. If it were in my power, your sister would be returned to you with a fat stack of cash for her trouble."

"You're a devil," she says, smirking at me and turning to face me. I return it.

"A devil who's grateful," I say in a husky tone, and

I take a step closer to her. She doesn't step back, but her shining eyes look up at me meaningfully.

The adrenaline from the car chase is still pumping through our veins, and I know she can feel it in her pounding heart. We've both been through a lot the past couple days, and I haven't had any privacy in jail.

The look on her face says a thousand words that all contradict each other. Part of her wants to shoot me, and part of her wants to kiss me.

"I've been taken advantage of too," I say in a deep whisper. "And I don't appreciate it. Through it all, one person has offered me help: you. The one person who I should hate the most," I add, taking her chin between my thumb and forefinger.

Her lip curls up, and her eyes get lidded. "Thinking of taking your chance?" she asks. "Take me down right here in a soundproof room, get my gun from me, take the car keys, and rocket off out of state?"

"Not a bad plan," I admit. "But I have a better one."

I wrap my hands around her hips and press a kiss into her. She gasps, pressed back against the wardrobe, and I lean into her.

It's hot and fierce, and as soon as we're together again, it's like something dormant comes back to life. The room is silent except for our groaning, but our bodies feel like they're on fire.

She twists and squirms, and I think she's trying to get away, but I realize she's working her shirt off. I help her with the buttons and slide the blouse off, and I waste no time in getting her bra unhooked and tossing it aside as well.

With her breasts free, I pick her up and roughly toss her onto the bed a second before I'm on top of her.

There's no need to take things slow or pace ourselves. We both know we want each other, and god knows I need the release. My touch on her is rough and animalistic. I grope her breasts as we kiss again, and my tongue invades her mouth. In jail, the touch of a woman is something that makes you long for release more than anything. It consumes your thoughts when you let yourself get idle.

"I thought about you while I was in there," I growl once our kiss breaks and my mouth goes to her ear. "All that time, you knew you were the last person I was with. You liked that, didn't you?"

"Maybe I did," she gasps, a smile forming on that mouth of hers.

"And you call *me* the devil," I growl, and I pinch her nipple. She gasps, and I reach around her back and slide my hand down until I feel metal.

Her eyes spring open when she realizes I'm holding her gun.

For a split second, the thought of taking advantage of this situation crosses my mind. She was right, it should be what I do. She took advantage of me in bed last time, so this is only fair payback. We lock eyes for a moment, then I slide the pistol out and set it on the nightstand.

"I'm surprised," she says, a faint smile crossing her lips.

"I am too," I say, and I silence her with a kiss. I put my hands to her face, cupping her head as I relish the feeling of her soft lips against mine, and I grind my cock against her skirt.

The feeling of her skirt against me alone is enough to set me off. My cock is rock-hard and threatening to burst from my pants as I grind against her until her skirt is bunched up past her thighs.

I reach down to her panties and tug them down. She thrusts her hips up to let me get them down past her knees, then off her legs altogether. Once they're out of sight, I don't even check to see where they ended up before I pull her whole body to the edge of the bed and shove my face between her legs.

My grip around her hips is tight, and I don't give her a single moment to prepare before I bring my face to her pussy.

Her scent is heady and full of need, and I've never craved anything in my life like I've craved her. I let my tongue out and let it roll over the warm surface of her lips, and I taste that she's almost ready.

"I've been on your mind too, it seems," I growl, and she tries to clench her legs around my head.

"Fuck you," she gasps, but there's mirth in her voice, and I grin before I let my tongue touch her pussy again.

I go deeper this time, then deeper, and each time I part her lower lips with my tongue, I feel her body responding to me sweetly. She twitches and gets hotter, her hips twist this way and that, and her legs squirm, but my hands have an iron grip on her. I let her move, but only enough that she knows who's in control.

Once I start really tasting the honey that she starts giving me, I can't hold myself back. The tip of my tongue darts to her clit, and once it starts striking it, I don't stop. I go again and again and again, pushing her soft lips apart to get to that sensitive nub that electrifies her every time I toy with it.

It's like I have a key to turning her senses up, and I'm relentless with it.

It isn't long before I feel her start to get tense, a tension that starts right above the nub I'm torturing and runs all the way up her abdomen.

I tighten my grip around her hips, and she puts her hands into my hair to hold on tight as she arches her back.

"God, god, Misha, ohhh!" Each word comes with a breath of pure desire, and each syllable pushes her closer to the edge. My tongue lashes out again and again until I feel the tension reaching its breaking point.

Nicole tosses her head back, and her legs wrap around my head as she throws her own head back and lets out a long, desperate gasp of release. My face feels wet, and I my chest groans as I let out a long, low rumble.

She hasn't even finished coming when I stand up from her. She opens her eyes, panting and looking up to me desperately with pleading eyes.

I kick my shoes off, and my pants come next. My cock sticks straight out, bulging and ribbed with veins that long to be inside her.

I run my hand up and down my shaft, and I feel like a vessel that's utterly full and ready to pour itself out. And the look in Nicole's eyes tells me she's more than ready to be that vessel for me.

I crawl onto the bed on my knees, and she crawls back until she's at the headboard — a large panel with a red cushion to pad it. She puts her arms over her head and holds on tight to the fake gold as I reach her, clasp her hips, and enter her.

There's no hesitation, no caution, and no inhibitions. I thrust myself up into her, raw, and she receives me like a welcome guest, slick and hot and wet as I remember her when she was Misty to me.

She lets out a delighted sigh as soon as I'm inside her, but I silence that with a hot, fierce kiss as I start bucking up into her.

My cock is swollen to the point that I feel like I could release at any second, all for her. The soft underside of my shaft runs smoothly against her wet insides, and I feel the tip of my cock grinding up against her in soft, sweet ecstasy. My whole body is coming back to life. Everything in this mountain of a body of mine feels like it hasn't truly been out of jail yet until touching her.

And I'm going to make sure she knows she's mine.

I start rutting into her like our lives depend on it. I'm holding nothing back. From the very start, I come in fast and hard, pounding her against the headboard in such a way that she gets shoved up against it with each thrust of my hips.

Every sit-up I did, every minute of exercise in my massive body, it was all thinking of her.

My hands work her hips as I thrust like a precise piston over and over again, but even so, she's able to keep up, thrusting her own hips in tandem with mine. I get to know what she really desires, how much of her she wants me to take and ravish until we've had our fill of each other.

And the way she's moving, I know she has one hell of an appetite for me.

My ceaseless thrusting starts to get her wound up again, and I feel her tightening around me. I start to let myself go without a second thought, and I've never wanted to release myself into someone so deserving and so passionate.

My head is swimming by the time we've reached

the peaks of our tension, like two bolts of lightning crossing. I've never felt this way about anyone. Maybe it's the adrenaline, maybe it's how fucked up my mind is after weeks on end without release, or maybe Nicole is just an astounding woman, but everything in my pounding body is working in perfect harmony and ferocity toward one goal: making her thrash and moan in ecstasy.

And seconds later, that's exactly what I feel.

Nicole's face goes red, her mouth falls open, and she loses her grip on the headboard as her whole body starts to shake and writhe. I hold her up and bring my lips to hers to kiss her passionately while she comes, and at the same time, I feel my balls tighten and fire run up my shaft as I start to release inside her.

The feeling of our two bodies pulsing together, coming to that beautiful, higher state of mind in a shared orgasm is like nothing I've ever experienced before. So much seed spills out of my cock, burst after burst, that I'm even surprised at myself. Our hearts are beating faster than ever before, and my whole body feels like it was made for this.

We haven't stopped thrusting. It makes my body burn, but it's so sweet that nothing could stop me. Each thrust draws out our orgasms so much more, makes us both feel so relaxed and breathless that we could do it until we pushed ourselves past our limits.

After what feels like an eternity, the whitc-hot

passion dies down, and we're left with just the sound of our breaths as our kiss breaks.

My cock is still hard as a rock.

I slide it in and out of her a few times, slowly, letting her feel me between her legs in this state of oversensitive afterglow. She lets her head fall back against the wall, and she breathes deeply, mouth hanging open.

She looks like a masterful painting.

"I missed you," I confess in a dark, husky tone, and her eyes flutter open.

"I missed you too," she admits, shame and pleasure in her voice together as she smiles. She lets out a long sigh as I draw my cock out of her, and she slides under the sheets with me as we press ourselves into each other.

My lips touch her cheek, and I reach down to rub her clit with two fingers to wind her down.

She smiles, her body beginning to relax, a purr coming from her throat that's cut off by a scream when there's a sudden bang, and the room door crashes open.

Iinstinctively grab the bedsheets coiled up at the end of the bed and yank them up over my mostly-naked body, ducking down and looking around for some kind of weapon. Anything at all I can wield against our attacker. I reach out and grab the bedside lamp, ripping the cord out of the wall in my haste to defend myself.

Misha is on the exact same page, only luckily he has already pulled his boxers back on and is therefore able to quickly jump up into a fighting stance. All traces of the tender, passionate man he was a few moments ago have vanished, leaving only this well-trained warrior in its place.

The door flings back against the wall so hard it makes the bed rattle, dust showering down from the ceiling like snow. It takes me a full few seconds to register what image is unfolding in front of me. The first aspect I notice is a gun. The round metallic holes of the barrel aimed straight at my face. I follow the long snout of the rifle up to the surprisingly feminine hands, the finger poised on the trigger with a manicured nail.

And from there, my eyes roll up the plaid flannel-clad arms and narrow shoulders, the pale face of the marksman with one eye closed and framed with crow's feet while the other squints through the sight of the rifle at Misha and me.

Our attacker is smaller than expected, barely my height. She is thin and willowy, with a shock of shoulder-length auburn curls popping out at odd directions all over her head. Something deep inside me swells with nostalgia, with recognition of a figure I have barely thought about, much less visited in the flesh for many years.

"Mom?" I gasp, lowering the lamp clutched in my right hand. Slowly, the closed eye opens and the woman pulls her face away from behind the rifle, still holding it up, pointed at us. At first she only squints and grimaces, as though she can't trust her own eyes to tell the truth. Like she's having some wild hallucination and is desperately trying to find her footing in this shaken-up, upside-down universe. Misha glances back and forth between us, even more confused than either of us combined, trying to put two and two together. He cautiously lowers his fists, but doesn't relax completely. He steps closer to the bed, shielding me slightly with his arms.

"What in the world," she murmurs, her cinnamon-brown eyes going wide and her mouth falling open. She slowly lets the rifle fall down to rest at her side. She raises one hand to clap over her mouth, shaking her head in pure disbelief.

"What's going on?" Misha growls, looking at the woman in the doorway, then back at me. I shake my head, totally stunned to see this blast from the past. The woman standing in front of us looks somehow like a total stranger and yet so familiar and almost comforting that it makes me want to cry.

"What are you doing here?" I ask, wrapping myself more tightly in the sheets.

She scoffs.

"Me? What am *I* doing here? What the hell are *you* doing here?" she retorts, throwing up her free arm in indignation.

"Oh no, you do not get to be the one asking questions," I shoot back, glaring at her.

"I find you naked in bed in a brothel with some jacked-up thug and you want to act all high and mighty with me?" my mother quips. She puts her hand on her hip and raises an eyebrow at me. "You're on *my* turf right now, little lady, and you better start spilling."

"Your turf?" I scoff, getting up and hastily pulling on my shirt and skirt haphazardly, my anger starting to get the best of me. "Mom, this is a legal brothel. My friend used to work here years ago and I— wait, why am I telling you any of this? It's not like you care."

My mother winces and looks away, her jaw tightening with anger and hurt. That comment seems to sting a little more harshly than I intended, and for a moment I consider taking it back and apologizing. But in the end, my stubbornness overrides any pity I feel for my mother. After all, she's the one who abandoned me, not the other way around. I don't owe her anything — not an apology, not an explanation, nothing.

"You know that's not true, Nicki," she says softly. I feel myself inwardly flinch a little at the sound of her old nickname for me.

"It's Nicole. Or *Officer* Burns. Nobody calls me Nicki," I reply, folding my arms over my chest. Misha lays a hand on my shoulder, grounding me. I glance up at him. He has a stony, detached look on his face. I can tell he knows not to interfere right now. This isn't his battle, and it sure as hell isn't really his business, but it's still nice to have him standing behind me, just the same.

My mother walks into the room slowly and I brace myself, though for what I don't know. She strolls over and gently, carefully sets the rifle down on the corner table, then turns back to face me with an almost pleading look on her face. I instantly feel awash in a sea of guilt. She has always had that ability, to make me feel bad about my choices, even though god knows between the two of us, I'm not the one notorious for bad decisions.

"Officer Burns," she murmurs, feeling out the words. There's a slight quiver to her voice, her cheeks going splotchy like they always have before she cries. It's funny how so much time can pass, and yet I can still predict her movements as well as ever before.

"Yeah. I'm a vice cop now," I tell her flatly. I refuse to let her emotions infect me. I'm not going to let her decide how this conversation goes — if there is to be a conversation at all.

"Just like your father," my mother says, biting her lip. She hastily wipes at her eyes before the tears can fall. "I always knew you'd do something worthwhile with your life."

That statement makes my heart swell, but I force myself to stay aloof. She can so easily unravel me, but I won't let her. Not this time.

"Yeah. If only you'd been around to see it," I remark, a little coldly.

"You're right. I screwed up, Nicki. Sorry. Nicole," she corrects herself. She sighs, running a hand back through her messy curls. "I have made a lot of stupid-ass choices in my life. Too many to count. But leaving you and Samantha… well, that is the decision I most regret. I should have been there all this time. For you and your sister."

"Yes. You should have," I agree firmly.

My mother stares at me hard, as though she's trying to soak up every little aspect of my appearance and demeanor, like she's been starving for the sight of me for all this time. I wonder if she's just trying to memorize my face so she can hold onto the image when we part. Which will probably happen sooner rather than later.

I brought Misha here because I thought it would be a suitable place to hide out, but there's no way we can make this work now. Not with my mother hanging around. Although I still have no earthly idea why she would be here in the first place.

Almost as though she's read my mind, she says, "I'm sure you are wondering why I'm here anyway. It's a long story."

"I'm sure it is. But we don't have a lot of time," I lie. Truthfully, I have no clue where else we could go to lie low if we leave here. It's not like I have a ton of safe houses tucked away just on the off chance that I end up hiding from the mafia or the law or whomever it is chasing after us and threatening our lives.

Then it hits me: my mother doesn't seem to know that Sam is missing.

I can't possibly leave here without telling her. But that kind of information isn't exactly the lighthearted tidbit I can just drop on her without warning. She looks tough and capable, but I have a feeling this bad news will hit her pretty hard. I don't want to completely decimate her.

I have to ease into it.

And that means I'm stuck here, at least long enough to catch up with my mother. It isn't the most pleasant prospect, but it's the right thing to do, and I know it.

Damn my internal moral compass. Just once I would like to ignore my conscience.

"You can't leave just yet," she pleads, taking a step closer. "I-I want to talk to you. Find out what I've missed out on. Clearly, I've missed a lot." She looks pointedly at Misha.

"Oh. This is kind of a new thing, actually," I admit awkwardly.

Misha steps up and offers his hand, still dressed in just his boxers. My mother's face flushes pink as she shakes his hand, and I can tell it's taking all of her willpower not to instinctively look him up and down, every inch of his gloriously powerful, chiseled frame.

"Misha," he says. "Nice to meet you."

"Nice to meet you, too, though I wish it were under better circumstances," Mom says. She leans around him to look at me, an expression of intense longing on her face. "You are so beautiful. And tough. I can't believe how different you look," she tells me quietly.

"Well, it's been a long time," I say, shrugging. "Years."

"I know. And I hate that it's been so long, sweetheart. I have messed it all up so many times I can't even count," she admits. "One thing is for sure. I have missed you every single day that we've been apart. I know you will never forgive me for walking out, but I just want you to understand how truly sorry I am. I hitched myself to the wrong guy, Nicole. I was stupid and grieving and reckless. Losing your father… well, it sent me spinning. And I guess after a while, I just spun out of control entirely. It took me a long time to find my footing again. And by the time I came back down to earth, I had already lost the two most precious parts of my life."

"I still don't understand why you did it, Mom," I confess, sniffling a little. "Why did you leave? I used to replay it over and over again in my head, trying to figure out what made you leave us. We needed you."

"I know, baby. I know that now. But at the time, I was so caught up in Darrell's bullshit. He had me in a damn trance, Nicole. I was terrified of him. Terrified to disobey or disagree in the slightest. I was blinded by fear and grief. You know, I never got over losing your father. Sometimes I wake up and not remember for a moment that he's gone. And then it hits me, and it's like I relive the pain all over again," Mom laments, a tear rolling down her cheek.

"I turned to Darrell for comfort. I wasn't used to being alone. I was a stay at home wife and mom my entire adult life up until the day your father died. I was so lonely that I made excuses for everything Darrell did. I put aside the bad things and amplified the good things. But you, you could see right through him from the very start. I think that's why it hurt so badly. Because deep down, I knew you were right not to trust him. Every time the two of you argued, I could feel my heart ripping apart. I held us together as long as I could, but…"

"In the end, you chose him," I murmur. "He walked out, and you walked out with him. I was just seventeen, and I had lost my father and my mother. You know, I warned you. I told you that if you didn't stay away from lowlifes like Darrell, you'd end up going the same way yourself. In the underworld, struggling to get by. Is that what happened?"

She nods.

"Yes. For months, I followed him from one rock bottom to the next, and just when I thought I couldn't sink any lower, I got this job here. I'm the house mother. At first, I was so embarrassed and ashamed to have fallen so far. But over time, I learned to love the work, to love my girls. It's selfish to say, but I think part of why I warmed to the job so much was that I just missed you and Samantha so much. I used my girls here as surrogates for you two. And after a year, I had finally saved up enough money to support myself. I kicked Darrell to the curb and I've been on my own ever since."

"Wow," I breathe, taking a few steps closer, still hugging my sheet to my chest. It's not really appropriate attire for a heart to heart, but she did bust in... unexpected. "You really did all that? You got rid of Darrell? Mom, I'm... I'm proud of you."

She smiles faintly, tears still misted over her eyes.

"It may not seem like much to most people, but I'm finally starting to learn how to stand on my own two feet. Without Darrell. Without your father. I'm no longer ashamed of my work here. I protect these girls. I love them like my own. The only thing missing from my life are my real daughters. That's why it's so wonderful to see your face again, Nicole. I can't tell you how badly I've missed you. I don't care what circumstances led you here. I'm just happy to have you standing in front of me again."

I can't stand it anymore. I rush forward and throw my arms around her, crying softly as she hugs me tight. Misha just stands back and lets the moment unfold.

I push back for a moment and ask, "But Mom, if you've been okay for so long, why didn't you reach out? Why didn't you track me down?"

"Oh, sweetheart. I was so embarrassed of how far I've fallen. Embarrassed of how rotten Darrell turned out to be. I really believed that you and Sam were better off without me dragging you down. And maybe I was right. I mean, look at you! Officer Burns! You did that all on your own. You never needed me," she explains tearfully.

"No, Mom. I do need you. I can survive on my own, but I still need my mother," I assure her, giving her another hug.

"Well," she sighs, beaming at the two of us, "I'll leave you to get properly dressed. Come downstairs when you're ready. And don't you sneak out. I've just got you back and I am not about to lose you again, Nicole."

"I promise we won't sneak out," I tell her, smiling.

She taps me on the nose, a look of intense affection in her eyes. She turns and leaves the room. Misha gives me a look of utter shock and I just wordlessly shrug. There are no words to sum up how bizarre this situation is, but Misha doesn't press me any further. We quickly get dressed and head back downstairs, where my mom is waiting with a beer for each of us. She pats the bar stool next to her and I sit down, taking a much-needed sip of beer.

"So, Mom, I hate to ask this, but why did you come barging into the room earlier? With a gun, no less?" I ask. She sighs.

"Well, I got word that there was an assault going on up there. One of our girls was in trouble, or so I heard. I was out getting supplies when I got the news. So I raced here to stop the assault," she admits, taking a long sip.

"Whoa. So you were literally about to shoot a guy for hurting one of your girls?" I ask.

She nods firmly.

"Yes. Absolutely. Without question. Or at least fire a warning shot to make him crap his pants and get his filthy hands off my girl."

"Damn, Mom. That's intense," I remark, a little impressed.

"That's the role of the house mother. I look after my little chickadees, whatever that may entail. I'm not afraid to show some muscle if it means my girls stay safe," Mom explains.

"Who told you there was an assault taking place?" pipes up Misha.

"Oh," she says, "I got a phone call."

I look at Misha, wide-eyed.

His face is grim and his voice is dangerous. "We're being watched."

"We have to go," I say simply as I watch the thoughts roll through Nicole's mind.

"Right," she agrees, snapping herself out of her trance. She looks up to her mom and gives a smile full of mixed emotions. "So…"

Her mom steps in and wraps her arms around Nicole, to her surprise, but Nicole quickly softens and smiles as she returns the gesture. I glance away to let the two have a moment, pretending to be interested in one of the big paintings on the wall.

"You stay safe, Nicole," she says in a quiet tone. "I don't want to lose you again, do you hear me? I know I can't really ask that kind of thing of you, but…"

"I get it, Mom," she says back. "Thanks. I will."

"I want to be in touch after all *this*," she gestures between me and Nicole, "gets settled, okay?"

Nicole opens her mouth to protest about whatever her mom thinks *this* is, but after a moment of silence, she just smiles and nods. "Alright, Mom. That sounds good." She turns to me, and I raise a single eyebrow at her. "Ready to go?"

"I'm driving," I say after a nod.

"He sounds fun," Nicole's mom says, and Nicole turns away from her as quickly as possible to make a brisk beeline to the door with a horrified look on her face. Her mother flashes me a smile, and I hold back a chuckle as I follow Nicole out the door.

Even as I step out into the Nevada desert sun and squint while Nicole makes her way to the car, though, I can't help but feel like I'm looking at a very different woman than either the stripper named Misty or the cop who arrested me.

"Keys," I call to her as we move to the doors, and I catch them after she tosses them to me.

"Hoping to show me up after I saved our asses on the way here?" she asks with a challenging undertone, but I just chuckle as we get into the car.

"Oh no, *officer*, I just watched you have a teary-eyed and heart-wrenching reunion with your mother. You don't get to act like a badass for at least twenty-four hours."

"Oh so there's rules on it, now?" she retorts,

crossing her arms, and I smirk as I pull out onto the road.

I try to keep reminding me that this woman betrayed me, but even as I do, I think back to the look on her face when she was telling me my rights at the arrest. It's was the same hurt, vulnerable woman I saw a few minutes ago being reunited with her mother, and it's the same one who's trying to put on a tough face in the passenger's seat right now.

This cop is proving to be a lot more than meets the eye, and for the first time in a long time, I'm not sure what to make of the feelings running through my head. I know I can't get her out of my mind, but I assumed it was just her body and the tension between us that was driving me wild. The more I look at her, though, the more I find myself wanting to get to know more about her.

Realizing that worries me.

"What?" she asks suddenly, snapping me out of my trance. I glance over at her. "You had a glazed look on your face."

"Oh, nothing," I lie. I need to keep this feeling in check. To say it would never work between the two of us would be an understatement.

She frowns and opens her mouth to ask more as I pull out onto the highway, but her phone lights up as she gets a call. She gives the number a worried look.

"Shit," she mutters. "It's the head of my unit."

"Sounds friendly," I joke.

"Keep quiet," she asks me, and I give a curt nod before she opens the phone.

"This is Nicole," she says. I can hear muffled chattering through the line, and I glance over every now and then to see Nicole's face wince.

"Sounds like you're on top of things," she says in a guarded tone. "But I did everything I could on the stand, and you know it. That evidence was gone, and you can check the security tapes to prove that I wasn't anywhere near it the night before the hearing."

Her face slowly melts from frustration to wide eyes and shock, but her tone stays even.

"I see. Well then, let's pull the tapes and-"

The voice from the other end of the line gets more agitated, and I watch Nicole's face go pale. She clenches her fist for a moment before pinching the bridge of her nose. "Sir, I need more time. I was the arresting officer. Without me, at this stage in the investigation the-"

She clenches her jaw as her superior interrupts her again, and her glare could kill a man.

Finally, she gives a terse reply.

"I understand, sir," she says. "No, sir." She hangs up the call and holds herself back from hurling the phone out the window.

"Sounds like it went well."

"I'm suspended," she snaps, and I raise my eyebrows in genuine surprise.

"What? Why?"

"Not the reasons he gave, that's for damn sure," she says. "But I think this gives us a lead. He's accusing me of throwing my testimony on purpose, like you thought I did."

"I must admit, that's what it looked like to an outsider's perspective," I say. "My attorney was counting her blessings after that hearing."

"Yeah, but there's no way he didn't know that evidence really was missing," she says, leaning forward and furrowing her brow. "When things like this happen, suspending the investigating officer usually isn't the first step someone takes."

"Smells rotten to me," I say, and she nods.

"Me too. The way he was talking, I think he was mocking me," she adds with a frustrated sigh. "Bastard probably knows I know the truth and is just holding it over my head. He had something to do with all this. He's throwing me under the bus so fast it's got to be to keep attention off whatever's really going on."

I am silent for a few moments, nothing but the noise of the engine and the wheels on the asphalt to soften the silence in the car.

"I just can't fucking believe this," she says, glaring out the window. "After everything I do for that department, this is how they thank me. Letting me be some throwaway pawn in whatever it is they're up to."

"They always target the strongest enemy, when power is shifting around," I say in a calming tone, and she raises an eyebrow at me. "You should take it as something of a compliment. They're afraid of you, so they don't want you around. You took down Misha Chaykovsky, after all," I add with a smirk.

That teases the shadow of a smile to her lips, but she looks away from me.

"Well, at least I've got all the time in the world to think it over," she says ruefully. "Where are we going, anyway?"

"Back to the club," I say. "In Vegas. I have a contact there who owes me a favor, and I think this is just the time to call that favor in."

"Let me guess," she says with the faintest groan, "another battle-hardened Russian killing machine standing at just under seven feet tall and able to break a neck without increasing his heart rate?"

"Something like that," I say with a smile.

* * *

THE LOOK on Nicole's face a few hours later when I point to the stripper in the club's dressing room is priceless.

"You're kidding," she says flatly as Tatiana turns and looks at us in surprise.

"Misha!" she calls, a smile spreading across her

face as she gets up and comes over to us. "Good god, I thought you were still…?"

"Not as of today," I say with a calm, confident smile. "Good to see you again, Tatiana."

The woman standing in front of us is barely over five feet tall, and couldn't look further from the image Nicole was imagining in the car.

"You two know each other?" Nicole asks us, a single eyebrow raised in surprise.

"Yes," I say. "Just over business matters, nothing special."

"By 'nothing special', he means I owe him my life," Tatiana says to Nicole. "Let's just say that if Misha here hadn't been so willing to help me, I'd be back in Russia a lot worse off than I am now. I'm in a bit of trouble back home, so I don't plan on going back anytime soon." Her tone is lighthearted despite how severe the reality is.

She's wanted for treason back in Moscow, and the strings I pulled are the only reason she hasn't been deported yet.

"I wanted to drop by with this new friend of mine first thing," I say, nodding to Nicole while looking at Tatiana. We're alone in the dressing room, but we won't be for long. "And you can relax, Tatiana, Nicole is working with us, for the time being. Let's go to the VIP lounge, shall we?"

Once we have our privacy, sitting on the black velvet sofas of the luxurious room with its gleaming blue chandelier hanging overhead, I pace around the room slowly while Nicole and Tatiana take seats across from each other.

Tatiana is a new hire at my club, but I know exactly what kind of person I'm dealing with. She's sharp and attentive, and she has a knack for getting out of danger. There's nobody else in the club I can trust and rely on as much as her right now.

"So, tell me," I start. "What have the vultures been whispering since I got put away?"

"You know I don't like to listen in where I'm not welcome," Tatiana lies coyly, and I crack a smile, but Nicole's eyes are unreadable as they move between the two of us. "But since you asked, it hasn't exactly been hard to pick up on a few things from the dressing room."

I stand behind Nicole's couch, putting my hands on the back of it to watch Tatiana expectantly.

"Getting put behind bars wasn't good for your public image around here," she says, crossing her legs and putting her arms back over the couch. "That much is for sure."

"Do people really think someone like Misha would talk to the police," Nicole says in disbelief, half-laughing, but I shake my head down at her.

"It doesn't matter what kind of man I am," I say. "Going to jail means I'm a hidden element. The *bratva* doesn't like when it can't see what's going on. Being out of the game like that for any amount of time means I *could* talk to the police, and that alone puts a target on my back."

Nicole's face reddens a bit. I know she feels guilty by now over what she did. I'm surprised by my impulse to put a hand on her shoulder and reassure her, but I hold it back. Now is the time for business.

"So, people are whispering about me already?" I ask Tatiana, and she nods.

"We had some heat on us right after you were arrested. Couple of raids on other clubs, but they didn't turn up anything serious. I don't think the cops were looking for anything — just trying to show the *bratva* that they're watching. It's made everyone anxious." Tatiana's eyes flit to Nicole for a moment. "Your friend here hasn't helped, I'm afraid."

Nicole shifts in her seat. "How so?"

"People say Misha is thinking with the wrong head," Tatiana admits reluctantly, gesturing between her legs, and I roll my eyes. "They'd never say it to his face, of course, but having your sister kidnapped makes it look like the two of you are closer than many of the ambitious *bratva* soldiers are comfortable with. I'm surprised you're even here, honestly."

"She's here because I didn't order her sister taken," I say, and Tatiana's eyes widen. "I was informed of it, but I never gave word, implicitly or otherwise."

"Now that is interesting," Tatiana says, leaning forward. "Because that's not what's going around the rumor mill. The way people are talking, it sounds like the two of you are just dropping everything for some romantic lover's adventure, fights and all."

"Someone's making it look like we're burning all our bridges left and right," Nicole says, realization coming over her face."

"So when they make a move and kill the two of us," I say casually, "there will be no repercussions on either side. We'll just be a couple of loose ends someone buries out in the desert and does both the LVPD and my mafia a favor while they rake in all the winnings."

"Christ," Nicole says. "I've been setting these mousetraps my whole career. So this is what it feels like to be caught in one."

I make my way to the bar and pour us a round of vodkas on ice, as calm and collected as ever. "The difference is that in a working mousetrap, the victim doesn't know what's coming for him." I hand the glasses to the girls and lock eyes with Nicole. "But we do."

"We don't know *who* it is, though," she says. "I've got a gut feeling about my superior on my end, but…"

"Patience," I say. "Our enemy doesn't know we're onto them yet. That's something you use to your advantage, isn't it?"

Nicole smirks and takes a drink, eyeing me.

"So, what do you suggest?"

"If we split up, we're dead," I say. "I will be, at least. They'd have to be very careful before killing a cop, even one who's on unpaid suspension. As long as you're with me, my odds are a lot better, so I'm keeping you by my side."

"Keeping me now, is it?" she asks with a challenging raise of her eyebrows.

"Unless you'd rather take your chances on your own, knowing there's a *bratva* coup being set up that depends on you taking part of the fall," I offer with a playful shrug of my shoulders. She glares at me, but she nods.

Tatiana is glancing between us, probably uncomfortable with the various kinds of tension even I can feel crackling between me and Nicole right now. But she says nothing, and Nicole and I don't break eye contact for a long time.

"So, what do you say, officer?" I say, sitting down on the table in front of her and leaning forward with a smug smile. "Haven't you always wanted to take down some *bratva* heavy hitters?"

"Well, let's see," I reply thoughtfully, scratching at my chin. "I'm suspended without pay from the job I have clawed my way into and given my heart and soul for years. My sister is missing, compliments of the Russian mafia. I just found out my long-lost mother has been within a hundred miles of Las Vegas all this time, running the same legal brothel my old friend used to work at. And I've spent the better part of the day driving around the desert with a nearly-convicted criminal."

"So? What do you think? What is our next move, Officer?" Misha asks pointedly, emphasizing the last word. I get a strange thrill out of hearing him call me by my title. I don't know if it's pride, amusement, or arousal. Maybe all three. Who knows? It's been one hell of a weird day. Tatiana pats me on the shoulder and gives me a smile.

"Let me think for a moment," I reply, running my fingers back through my hair.

"You're one of the good ones, I can tell," she says earnestly. "I don't trust most of the policemen who come trolling through the club, but you're different. I just know it."

"She is different," Misha agrees, and I feel that same thrill once again. I need to get ahold of myself. I can't let my emotions take control right now. There's just too much going on. I don't have time for silly butterflies in my stomach. This is serious business.

"Well, I need to get back out on the stage before Matushka Galina starts wondering where I am. She can be really sweet when she wants to be, but my god is she cruel when she's angry," Tatiana says, rolling her eyes. "It was good to see you again, Misha, and not behind bars. Nice to see you, too, Misty," she adds with a wink and a giggle.

I blush hotly and give her a little wave as she flounces out of the dressing room, leaving the two of us standing there awkwardly. "I wonder if I'm ever going to live down being Misty," I comment. "I was only her for a few weeks, but it seems like Misty is a lot more popular than Nicole is."

"If it's any consolation, I'm starting to really admire Officer Burns. Although, Misty does have the considerable advantage, since she gave me a lap dance," he replies coolly.

There it is again. That flutter in my gut, the skip of my heart. Why in the world is this rough-edged, troublemaking criminal wiggling his way into my affections? Why is my own body betraying me? Every time he so much as looks at me, it's all I can do not to throw my arms around him and kiss him. I've already slept with the enemy more times than I should have.

Although, with the police force turning on me and the Bratva turning on Misha, I'm starting to rethink my alignment in all this. Who *is* my enemy, really?

Is it Misha? The thump-thump of my heart tells me otherwise.

"Anyway," I say, clearing my throat and changing the subject, "we need to get out of here. And since all eyes are focused on the two of us, from both sides, we need to go somewhere safe. Somewhere secluded, unsuspicious. A place where no one will come looking for us."

"All the safe houses I know of are under strict surveillance by the Vegas chapter of the Bratva. So my usual haunts are off-limits this time, I'm afraid," he explains gruffly. He's trying not to belie his true feelings about how grim this all is, about how betrayed he probably feels.

After all, the very brotherhood to which he has

dedicated sweat, blood, and years of his life have now turned their back on him purely for his dalliance with me. I feel a pang of regret and guilt again. I am the one who put him in jail. I am the one who slept with him and made him a target. I am the reason his family has turned on him.

And now, I may be the only one who can keep him alive.

So, wherever we go, we will have to go together. But where can we go where we won't be followed or watched?

An idea occurs to me. A good idea, possibly, although definitely unpleasant. I take Misha by the arm, looking up into his handsome face. "Come on," I tell him quietly. "Let's talk in the car. I know you have allies here, but I don't know if we trust them all anymore. Not to mention how many vice cops come through those doors. We could be being watched right now."

It's a chilling thought. Suddenly, I need to get out of there *now*.

The two of us exit through the back entrance and sneak back out to the car. This time I slide behind the wheel before Misha gets a chance to. He sighs and rolls the passenger seat much farther back, giving himself more room for his long legs.

"Should've done that in the first place," he remarks, looking much more comfortable and less squashed than he did when he first got into my car earlier today. "So, where are we headed next, Officer Burns? This time I'll follow your lead."

I glance over at him, taking in the angular lines of his face, the dark stubble shadowing his jaw. The sun is starting to descend across the horizon, drenching the world around us in hazy bronze light, fading quickly. Soon, it will be night, and we need to be safely tucked away somewhere by then.

"We're going to a place that I hoped never to experience again. It's hell for a police officer, but probably closer to heaven for two fugitives on the run," I explain vaguely. I'm admittedly a little hesitant to tell him where we're going. I'm not excited about it, that's for sure.

I thrust the key into the ignition and we pull off onto the strip, riding along as quickly and efficiently as possible. I'm trying to remain calm, but I'm also a little paranoid that we might run into one of my fellow cops out here on the streets.

Late afternoon seems like it should be a slow hour for policing, but in Vegas, that's not the case. The closer it gets to evening, the more lively the city gets. The desert sun is displaced by flashing neon and blinding headlights. The night owls of the city wake up and roll out of bed, mischief on their minds.

Every beat cop starts out training in these hours, and by sunset the streets are teeming with cops on the lookout for gamblers, thieves, drunks, and troublemakers.

"I never thought I would say these words to anyone, but you might not want to speed so much," Misha remarks. "We want to avoid getting the attention of the police."

"I know, I know. I'm just anxious to get a move on," I reply. "The strip is the last place we should be right now."

"You still haven't told me where we're going," he says.

"I need to get us out to the very edge of the city limits, to a place just barely outside of the jurisdiction of the Las Vegas police department. It's a hellhole, and a thorn in the side of all local vice cops because it's technically outside of our reach. Which, of course, only makes it a shining beacon for the area's seediest people," I begin, unable to hide my disgust.

"Sounds lovely," Misha comments sarcastically.

"Yeah. If you're a drug dealer or something," I answer.

"Hey now, you and I are on the wrong side of the tracks now ourselves," he says.

"Ugh. I know. Don't remind me. This is definitely not the trajectory I saw my career following when I first set out to be a police officer," I sigh.

"I hope I'm not crossing a line by saying this, but it sounds like they haven't been treating you as well as they should," Misha points out. "Why work so hard for people who don't appreciate you?"

I bite my lip, completely stumped on how to answer his point. Then I reply, "Well, I could ask the same of you."

"Easy answer. They're family."

"You said they would kill you if I don't stay with you," I remind him. "That doesn't sound like something family would do. Plus, I mean, you've just met my mother. Family isn't always all it's cracked up to be."

"Fair enough," Misha says.

We ride in relative silence for the remainder of the drive, and we reach the seedy hotel just before sunset. As I park the car, Misha gives me a dubious look. "Here? Really?" he asks.

"Yup. The Prickly Pear Motel. Home and hideout of Las Vegas's sketchiest inhabitants," I announce, with mock ceremony.

"It'll do," he agrees, getting out of the car. I head to the front desk to pay for a room on the night. The receptionist is a crusty old man with bushy white eyebrows and a jagged, pale scar running down his right cheek. He looks physically incapable of producing a smile, and if he's worked here as long as it seems, then I understand why.

"How many nights?" grumbles the man. His name tag reads *Ray*.

"Just one for now," I answer haltingly.

Ray nods slowly, swiveling around in his chair to grab a sheet of paper from the unruly stack teetering behind him on a shelf. My desk at the police department is meticulously organized, and seeing this cockroach-friendly, dusty, disorganized little office is just about enough to give me a panic attack. Ray moves at a glacial pace, plucking up the little reading glasses on a cord around his neck and settling them on his face so he can squint at the sheet of paper. He grimaces, clearly having trouble reading it. Then finally he sets it down in front of me and hands me a pen.

"Fill out your information," he grunts.

"Thanks. Okay," I mutter, taking the pen. I start trying to fill in a fake name on the line, but the pen doesn't work. Damn it. I look up at Ray with a sheepish smile. "The pen is out of ink."

He looks at me for a moment silently, like the cogs are turning ever so slowly in his head. Then he takes back the pen and paper and shrugs. "Don't worry about the paperwork then. Doesn't matter anyway. What floor you want?"

"Uh. I don't think it matters. First floor?" I ask.

Ray looks at the row of keys still hanging on the wall. He barks, "No vacancies on the first floor right now."

"Oh. Second floor, then?" I pipe up.

Again, he glances at the keys. Then he shakes his head. "No vacancies on second floor."

"Third floor?" I sigh.

"Yep. Got one. Here ya go," he grumbles, sliding a

rusty key across the counter to me. "That'll be forty bucks."

I start rummaging through my purse. "Do you take debit—"

"Cash only," he barks.

"Ah. Okay. Of course," I murmur, pulling out what little cash I have on hand. I never carry much cash, and I know Misha has nothing, since he's just come from the jail. I lay out three tens, a five, and a whole handful of assorted coins on the counter, blushing furiously.

Reminders of my time as Misty.

Ray eyes the stack of crumpled bills and coins with a look almost akin to disgust. Then he shrugs. "Close enough. Room 336. Have a wonderful stay. Check out is at noon."

"Thank you," I say, hurrying out of the office with a shudder. Misha's waiting for me, leaning against the wall, looking every bit the part of a bad boy. I hold up the keys and beckon for him to follow me up the two flights of rickety metal stairs to the third floor. After some time finagling the much-rusted key into the lock, we step into the room. It is surprisingly a little cleaner than expected, though the decor probably hasn't been changed since 1977.

"Not the worst place I've slept," Misha comments, walking straight toward the bathroom. He turns back and gives me a meaningful look. "I'm going to shower off if you want to come."

I blush, my eyes widening. The double entendre in his statement hits me like a ton of bricks to the face. "Oh. Um. I don't think—"

"The offer stands," he interrupts with a roguish grin. He closes the bathroom door and turns on the shower, leaving me standing in the middle of the cramped hotel room, internally arguing with myself. I look around the room, wrinkling my nose. At least the sheets look as if they've been washed in the last decade, which is a shock. I turn on the TV, but all I get is static, so I promptly turn it back off. With a sigh, I set my purse down on the bed and strip out of my clothes.

Well, there's certainly nothing better to do, I think to myself.

I step into the bathroom and close the door, feeling the steam wash over me. I can see Misha's tall, powerful frame silhouetted through the thin white shower curtain. He turns toward me and peeks out, his dark hair curling in the moisture. He gives me a broad smile.

"Yeah, yeah, I can't resist. You know I can't," I groan, rolling my eyes as I step into the shower with him. I sidle under the hot water and Misha enfolds me in his strong arms while the water soaks through my hair and slides deliciously down my back.

"I know everything is a fucking mess right now," he says in a low voice. He's stroking my hair, holding me close. "But I promise you that we will figure it all out. We are in this together now, Nicole. For better or for worse."

I look up at him with genuine gratitude. "Thanks. I didn't realize how badly I needed to hear that," I reply softly.

He leans in and kisses me gently at first, then harder, his tongue pushing into my mouth. I moan into his touch as he slides one hand down between my legs. He strokes my clit while he kisses me, and before long my knees are buckling. Without a word, Misha drops to his knees, hitching one of my legs over his shoulder while he devours my pussy. I cry out and fling my arm out to brace myself against the shower wall. I toss my head back and close my eyes, giving into the sensations as Misha's tongue flicks over my clit, bringing me closer…

"Oh my god," I gasp. "Misha!"

I climax with a powerful shudder, and Misha holds me in place, not letting up for even a moment. I come again and again in his mouth while the hot water pelts down my body. Then, while I'm still recovering, he stands up and kisses me again.

I can feel his cock hard and long against my thigh, and I can't help but reach for it. I begin to stroke him, listening to the way his breath hitches with every slide and touch of my hand. He presses into me, tangling his fingers in my hair and tilting my head to one side.

Misha leans in and kisses the side of my neck, the

ticklish spot just under my ear. He grazes his teeth delicately across my skin, making me shiver with pleasure. Suddenly, all I want is his cock inside me. All the stress and tension in my body longs for release, and I know only Misha can give it to me.

"Fuck me," I whisper to him. "Please, Misha. I need this."

With an appreciative growl, he spins me around and I brace myself against the wall with both hands as he bends me over, his cock hard against my ass cheek. I grind back against him, eager to be filled. Without a moment of hesitation, he slides his cock inside my aching pussy, groaning as he grabs my hips.

I let out a moan and hold on for dear life while Misha rears back and shoves into me, pounding my slick hole harder and harder. He's being rough with me now, like he's finally realized that I can take it, I won't break in half if he uses my body the way he needs to. He thrusts into me again and again, his hands groping my ass. His cock strikes deep inside me, brushing into my g-spot with every thrust. I can feel my pleasure mounting, growing and growing until I whimper and come again, gushing all over his hard cock.

"Fuck, you feel so good when you come," Misha growls. "Come again for me, *lapochka*."

He picks up the pace, slamming into me so hard that it almost hurts. I give in to the waves of overwhelming pleasure, my eyes watering as I shudder through yet another orgasm, drenching his cock with my sweet honey. With a few more powerful thrusts, Misha holds my hips tightly and comes inside me with a groan.

It's so deliciously sinful, and I wish my body didn't crave him like it does. But ever since I saw him at the stage, watching me, devouring me with his eyes, he's been under my skin. He's invaded all my thoughts, even with my world crashing down around me. He's the eye of the storm, and I don't want to let go.

When we're finished, I turn around and fold into his chest, resting my face against him while we come down from the rush.

We shower off quickly with the last remaining minutes of hot water, then wrap ourselves in towels and walk back out. I can see in the bathroom mirror that my hair is probably going to dry into a tangled mess, and my cheeks are flushed bright pink. But I feel a million times better. If I have to be on the lam, at least I'm on the run with the world's hottest partner in crime.

Still wrapped in a towel, I sit down on the bed and watch Misha get dressed. Then I see him take a small dark rectangle out of his pocket and I tilt my head to one side, confused. "What is that?" I ask, pointing.

He gives me a bemused look. "I know I fucked

you pretty hard, but are you really telling me you've forgotten what a cell phone looks like?" he teases.

I glare at him.

"Ha ha. Funny. No, I mean, where did you get that? Surely they didn't let you have a cell phone in the detention center?"

"No, of course not. My old burner got taken in for evidence. Which means it's probably conveniently 'lost' now along with the rest. But this is another burner I grabbed from the club while we were there earlier," he explains, as if it's the most normal thing in the world.

"What? How? When?" I ask, frowning. "I was right beside you the whole time."

He gives me a wink. "I'm good at my job, Nicole. I can be very subtle when I need to be. I keep burners stashed all over the place. This one was hidden in the dressing room."

"Wow. I didn't even notice," I admit, awestruck.

He turns on the phone and it beeps several times. The smile fades from his face and he walks toward the door. "Where are you going?" I ask.

"To listen to messages. I'll be right back in," he says quickly, stepping outside.

I sit nervously while he plays the messages, then he comes back in with a grave look on his face.

"What is it?" I inquire, getting up. Misha frowns.

"Nothing. Just… some new information I've been waiting on," he says cryptically.

"Well? You can't just leave it at that. Whatever happened to the two of us being in on this together, huh? What did you find out, Misha?" I press him.

"I found out more about your sister. My contact has informed me that she is, in fact, being held hostage. It's not a ruse. They're serious," he confesses.

"Shit," I murmur.

"No more waiting. We're going to do this my way now," he says, putting on his coat. I rush over and put my hands to his chest.

"No, wait. Let me… just let me call the police, okay?" I tell him.

"Nicole, we can't depend on them," he says. "These people do not want police involved."

"Please. Give me a chance. I-I know there's got to be someone at the station who will listen to me. Let me try," I say hastily, getting my phone out of my purse and dialing the number for the secretary.

"Hello, Vice," comes the cool answer.

"Hey, it's Nicole— Officer Burns. I need to report a missing person."

There's a heavy sigh. "Officer Burns, you're on suspension."

"I know, I know, but this is important. Just listen to me—"

"Lieutenant Harden said to defer your calls."

I stop suddenly. "What?"

"The lieutenant said to—"

"Yes, I heard you correctly," I snap. "But why?"

"It seems you're involved in something, uh, shady. I think that's the word he used."

Fuck. My boss has been spreading rumors about me. He really does have it in for me.

"Okay, well this is serious," I insist. "Listen to me."

There's a tone of pain in his voice when he says, "Nicole, if you have an emergency, you will have to dial 9-1-1 like anybody else."

"Are you kidding me?" I shout. There's a moment of silence.

"I'm hanging up now."

Click. I stare at the phone in disbelief for a few seconds. Misha doesn't say a word. I look over at him with tears in my eyes.

"They just… cut me out. Just like that. Like I'm just some common criminal or something," I breathe, still stunned. "I should have seen this coming. Look, I'll call 9-1-1."

I dial the number and spend a good ten minutes on the phone with the operator, who is more sympathetic, but also seems to think I'm crazy, spouting off some wild conspiracy about my kidnapped sister and the mafia and the vice department. I try my best to convince her, but she tells me there's nothing they can do.

I hang up, biting my lip and trying not to cry. I collapse back onto the bed and look up at Misha helplessly.

"I don't know what to do," I admit. Misha walks over to me and sets a huge hand on my shoulder.

"Like I said: we're going to do this my way now," he growls.

I stand up quickly and start to get dressed.

"Then I'm coming with you."

"No. No, Nicole. This isn't your territory. Let me handle this," he protests, shaking his head. I get dressed hurriedly, standing my ground.

"I'm coming, and that's final. Look, my sister is missing, and I don't have anyone else on my side but you. I am coming with you whether you like it or not," I tell him firmly.

He stares down at me for a moment, and I can tell he wants to say no. But to my surprise, he takes my hand and gives it a light squeeze.

"Okay," he agrees reluctantly. "But you'll follow my lead."

"…Wow," Nicole says as the two of us peer down into the trunk of my car. I have a smug look on my face, while her eyes are wide and staring at what she sees.

It's my arsenal.

I have a sniper rifle and its tripod, four Uzis, five 9mm pistols with silencers, two hand grenades, four hunting knives, a shotgun, a can of tear gas, and enough ammunition to keep them all firing for a long time. All of it is carefully and professionally stored in a hidden compartment in the bottom of my trunk, locked with a key.

It's after midnight, and I'm shining a flashlight down on it all to show Nicole before we get going. It's going to be one hell of a ride.

"If you're having second thoughts and care to arrest me," I say to her, "now's the time."

"I'll pass," she says, and I shut the trunk.

We pile into the car, I turn the ignition, throw the transmission into reverse, and we peel out onto the road, a trail of dust flying up behind us in a long stream.

"Why do you even have all that in the back?" she asks once we're on the road. "I thought hitmen were subtle."

"Subtlety has its place," I say casually. "For the other times, I like to be prepared."

"We're headed into the city," she points out as we move into the sea of towering casinos and bright lights."

"Yes."

"You said your contact told you Samantha was being held at some house in Blue Diamond, though."

"Yes."

She stares at me for a few moments before I raise an eyebrow at her and explain.

"We have to make a stop on the way."

"This isn't on the way," she points out.

"No, but we don't know exactly where in Blue Diamond she's being held. Unless you like the idea of just raiding every house in the town until we find her," I add, and she rolls her eyes.

"So what, we stop and chat up some more of your mysterious contacts to figure out what place she's at?"

"Not exactly," I say with a bloodthirsty smile. "I

have the names of the men who took her now, and I know the club they run. It's a Thursday night, so they'll be in the VIP room on their own. It's a real nice place, they've got one of those massive aquarium panels that takes up the whole wall of a room, and it casts this blue glow on everything."

I realize she's staring at me as I describe the place, and I give a light shrug. "I may be a killer, but I appreciate the finer things in life."

"I'm not sure a tacky aquarium wall counts as one of the finer things."

"That's why you're not a club owner," I remark with a wry smile, and she rolls her eyes at me.

We pull up in an alley behind the club. I normally need to be more cautious, but we're in a hurry tonight — caution is something we don't have time for. With a single streetlight flickering a few yards away from us, I pop the trunk open and start to arm myself.

A knife on each leg, two pistols at my side and one strapped to my chest, and an Uzi on my back. Nicole watches me get 'dressed' and raises her eyebrows.

"You look like you've gotten ready this fast a few times before."

"You don't get to be *pakhan* without being able to move fast," I say, then I nod to the trunk. "Take what you like."

She hesitates a few moments. I know she still has

some reservations about doing this. She was a cop until a few days ago, and I've tangled with enough cops to know it's in their blood, just like being *Bratva* is in mine.

I don't blame her for hesitating.

But if she wants to be doing things my way, she's going to have to get over it real fast.

"What would Samantha do?" I ask.

She looks me in the eye, nods, and picks up a couple of pistols for herself.

I slip my jacket back on to conceal my weapons once I'm armed, and Nicole does the same for herself. The weight of the weapons on me feels good with the weight on my chest gone.

This is the right thing to do, because I'm doing it for someone I care about. That much is clear to me now. I give Nicole one more look up and down once we're ready to head inside, and my heart pounds harder than it did while I was considering the worst possible outcomes of this fight.

"You look incredible," I say in a low husk, and taken by surprise, she smiles.

Before she can speak, I wrap my hand around the back of her neck and bring her into a deep kiss that she sighs softly into.

"Are you sure you want to be here for this?" I ask.

"Yes," she says, determination in her voice.

There's a lot to Nicole. Much more than I ever knew in the small woman I knew as Misty when I first brought her to my bed. Back then, I never would have guessed I'd be arming her and taking her to a firefight with me.

I certainly didn't think that after she arrested me.

Yet here we are, and there's nobody I'd rather have at my side.

"Let's go," I say, and she nods.

We circle around the block and head into the club.

It's not busy tonight, but it's not dead, which is perfect. The familiar sound of the music thrumming all around us and idle chatter around the club puts me at ease, and I notice Nicole relaxes a little bit too. She certainly did seem quite a bit happier stripping than she ever seemed as an officer, but considering our relationship... that could be explained by other things.

The bouncer doesn't give us a second glance as we stride in confidently, slipping through the sparse crowds.

We make our way across the club floor to the VIP lounge, where there's a bouncer eyeing us before we even get to the front. He doesn't recognize me fully until we're at the door, and his eyes start to widen as he does.

Before he can make a move for his radio, I slip my hand in my pocket and whip out a roll of $100s, glaring at him meaningfully. He freezes as we stand there, just a few inches from this whole raid getting exposed before we even get started.

"Three thousand," I say calmly. "Leave the radio and your phone, take a vacation for a few days. Everything behind that door won't matter in about five minutes."

The bouncer's jaw tightens, and he considers my words for a moment... then slowly takes out his radio and his phone and sets them of the table beside him. He takes my money, and without a word, he stalks out the door, not making eye contact with anyone.

I exchange a glance with Nicole.

"Can we trust him? she asks.

"No," I say, "which is why we'll be quick."

When I push the VIP room door open, my hand is already halfway through pulling out one of my pistols, and Nicole is right at my back.

As soon as we step inside, time feels like it's standing still for a fraction of a second.

Every eye turns to us.

The small party of Russians gathered there is all familiar to me. They're my lieutenants, my advisors, and a few of my business partners. All of them are men I've smiled with over drinks, shaken hands with, and had dinner with.

There are two strippers in the room, one of them standing at the bar holding two drinks and the other on the lap of my closest advisor. The only two souls who'll be spared this bloodbath.

To make things simple, I raise my pistol and put a bullet right through the head of my advisor, and just like that, the room erupts into chaos.

The first stripper ducks behind the bar while the second screams as part of my advisor's head gets blown off, and the other men reach for their guns and get up to take cover.

Shouts in Russian start flying through the room as I fire at the men and dive for cover behind one of the sofas, Nicole yelling at the dancers to get down. The sofa I chose has a man already ducking behind it, and I tackle him to the ground as I get down.

He punches me across the face, but I bring my forehead down on his nose and stun him long enough for me to deliver a quick strike to his neck that ends him while Nicole gives me covering fire overhead.

With two down in less than ten seconds, I take out my Uzi, and Nicole shouts down to me, "Give me cover!"

I sense what she's planning, and without a second thought, I put my trust in her, popping out of cover to rake a hailstorm of bullets on the men against the other side of the room. More specifically, I fire on the aquarium tank beyond it, filled with thousands of gallons of water. The glass cracks and shatters, terrifying the men in the room as water gushes out, and they dart away from the surging stream while Nicole runs out to the center of the room.

I fire on the fleeing men, dropping two of them while Nicole grabs the screaming stripper's arm and pulls her, heading for the bar where the first stripper is taking cover, and within five seconds, Nicole had gotten down with the two of them.

The floor is clear for me to do my work.

I vault over the couch and splash into the flooding water on the floor, spraying the couch across from me with my Uzi. I hear the cries of two men as the bullets penetrate the furniture and hit them.

One of them comes running out, clutching his wound and firing at me. A bullet grazes my arm before I put one of my own into his heart.

I keep running across the room, this time turning to a set of columns at the far end of the lounge where two more men are blind-firing my direction. I take cover behind the sofa and crouch down to run behind it to one of the columns, dropping my spent Uzi and pulling out a knife.

Whirling around the column, I catch one of the men by surprise and put a knife to his throat. I see the other man come out from his column to take aim at me, and I spin my hostage to use as a human shield just before he can get a round off.

The bullet goes through the man's neck and hits me in the shoulder. I clench my jaw, but adrenaline is coursing through me — I shrug off the pain.

I lift my pistol under the dead man's arm and fire at my attacker. The first round hits him in the chest, and he staggers back, into the open enough for Nicole to fire a round into the base of his neck and make him crumple.

I smile at Nicole, but it's short-lived. I see one of my *Avtoryet* charge forward, rushing her and raising his two guns.

I'm faster.

With two quick shots, I shatter his arms at the elbow and send him to the ground, splashing into the water and groaning in pain.

All around us, the room is filled with death and water as silence falls.

I slosh up to the man as Nicole holds the two dancers back, checking them to make sure they're unharmed. I seize a broken shard of glass from the aquarium and grab my former Avtoryet's collar, pulling him up and slamming him against the bar.

"No bullshit," I snarl at him, holding the glass to his throat. "Where is she? You know who I'm talking about. Make this easy, and I'll go easy on you."

"Why should I tell you anything?" he sputters, coughing blood.

"Because if you don't," I say, "I'll turn you over to her." I nod to Nicole, who's training a gun on him with fire in her eyes.

He hesitates for a few long moments, staring me

right in the eye until he finally growls, "2334 Park Lane in Blue Diamond. She's alone."

I drop the man, and he groans, curling up and holding his wounds.

I look to the strippers and nod to the exit for them to leave. They don't need to be told twice.

"Are you okay?" I ask Nicole as we head for the back exit, and she nods.

"Fine. You got shot," she points out, alarm in her face.

I grunt. "I'm still standing. Come on, we don't have much time."

We race out to the car and jump back in and start barreling west. It's not a short distance, which makes it even more nerve-wracking for Nicole as I fly down the highway to the sleepy little suburb where Samantha is.

It feels like the last few minutes didn't even happen, it was all so fast.

"We just left a room full of bodies back there," Nicole breathes, putting her hand on mine over the stick shift. The feeling of her warmth grounds me, and I give her a comforting smile.

"The world is better off without them," I say. "And don't worry about the man I questioned — he was bleeding out before I even touched him. He's a dead man. The only ones worth saving were the dancers, and they're fine."

She nods resolutely, staring toward the horizon and the town that's getting closer by the second.

When we pull up to the address, we waste no time. Weapons still at the ready, we spill out of the car and race for the garage side-door and stand at the ready by it.

One quick nod to Nicole says a thousand words before I turn and kick the door down.

The door flings open with a bang and Misha rushes into the garage, with me following close behind. It's dark in here, but with the light of Misha's burner phone we look around the room. It's still and quiet. There doesn't seem to be a single person here. My heart is still racing, but I can't figure out how I'm supposed to feel. It's like I've jumped on a rollercoaster, only for it to make an abrupt halt before the first big drop.

"What the hell?" I mumble, glancing around the shadowy corners of the empty garage. "Did we get the house number wrong? This can't be right, Misha."

"No. This is the right house," he says, shaking his head. "I'm certain of it."

"Then what is going on? Where is my sister? Where's Samantha?" I demand, starting to lose control. I thought we were so close. Everything has led us to this place, to this moment. I thought I was finally going to see my sister again.

"I don't know," he replies softly. "Something is very wrong here."

"You think?" I retort tearfully. "Your contact screwed us over, Misha! They lied to us! Who is your contact anyway? Just another lackey for the mafia? We were so stupid to trust them. We can't trust anyone."

"Calm down. We're going to find her," Misha assures me, but it's too late. I am falling into pure panic mode. I am exhausted and heartbroken and terrified. I don't know what has happened to my sister, I'm no closer to solving this mystery surrounding us, and now it looks like we've been duped.

"I bet they did this just to fuck with us," I mutter, swiping angrily at the tears burning in my eyes. "You might as well toss that burner phone off a cliff, because there is no one left in this world who can actually help us. Everybody has turned their backs on us. The mafia dropped you like a hot potato the second you became a liability. And whose fault is that? Mine! The police department has suspended me and won't even help me save my sister. And whose fault is *that?* Mine again! I've messed things up beyond repair."

"Nicole, stop. Beating yourself up is not going to

help us get any closer to solving this," Misha tells me. "You've got to hold yourself together. I will help you in any way I can. You may think everyone has turned their backs on you, but I won't do that. I won't abandon you."

"It doesn't matter," I murmur. Tears track down my cheeks as I shake my head. "We need to face it: we're outmatched here. Outmatched and outnumbered. It's like they're all five steps ahead of us every time."

"Then we will move faster. Think harder. We will race to catch up," he offers, walking over to me and pulling me to his chest. "This isn't over yet."

"Then why does it feel like we've reached the end of the line?" I ask, burying my face in his chest. He strokes my hair gently.

"Because this is a lot to take in all at once. But you and I are made of tougher stuff than these assholes expect. You're a vice cop in Las Vegas, for god's sake. I bet you're the only woman in your division, too."

I nod faintly. "I am."

"Exactly. And you know why? Because you're tough as nails. And you're smarter than any of them. They won't help you? Screw them! You don't need them, Nicole. You and I are going to find your sister and bring her home. We are going to make it," Misha says firmly. "But you cannot give up on me yet."

I take a deep breath and pull myself together,

wiping my eyes with the back of my hand. "You're right," I admit. "I'm sorry. I don't usually fall apart so easily. I just thought…"

"I know. You thought we'd find your sister here. But we've got to move on," he says.

I look around the garage one last time, and my eyes fall on something I hadn't noticed before: a rickety-looking chair in the corner of the room, with rope tied around it. I frown in confusion and walk toward it, pointing it out to Misha. "What's this here?" I ask, glancing back at him over my shoulder. He shrugs.

"Just a chair."

"No, but it's got ropes around it. Like there used to be someone tied up here," I comment.

"Well, there's no one here now, Nicole. We need to get out of here," he says.

"Just give me a second," I put him off, bending down in front of the chair, blinking in the near-darkness. I can make out something small and black on the seat of the chair, and as I reach for it, the screen lights up. It's a cell phone.

"What the hell?" Misha grunts, coming up beside me. I pick up the phone and let my eyes adjust to the brightness of the screen to read the word there. It's a name.

Samantha.

"Don't answer that," Misha warns, but before I can think twice, I slide the screen open to answer the call, pressing the phone to my ear with a shaky hand.

"H-Hello?" I whisper, scarcely able to breathe.

"Oh, it's all dark there! I can hardly see you!" giggles a lighthearted voice I would recognize anywhere, anytime. I hold the phone back to see that it's a Facetime call.

And my sister's smiling face is on the screen.

"Why are you sitting in the dark, weirdo?" she laughs. She's got her hair pulled back into a short ponytail, sunglasses on her head. Her face looks freckly and tanned, and she's grinning. There's patches of blue sky visible behind her, and the faint crash of waves on a shore.

"Sam?" I ask, shocked.

"Yeah, dummy! Of course it's me. Man, did I wake you up from a nap or something? You're acting weird. And why the heck didn't you tell me you got a new phone number! I've been trying to call you all day. Ilya — oh, that's my boyfriend — he said we should try to call you today and just fill you in on what's going on, but you wouldn't pick up!" she rambles brightly. She lifts a fruity drink to her lips and sips it through a straw.

"New number…" I murmur, confused. "Sam, what are you talking about? And where are you? Are you at the beach? The police think you're missing!"

"Missing? Oh, because I skipped some classes?" she says, rolling her eyes. "You know what, Ilya surprised me with a trip to Hawaii and I just couldn't say no. I mean, yeah, I might have to make up some exams when I get home, but how could I turn down a *free* trip to Hawaii? I'm sorry, I tried to call you, but for some reason it wouldn't go through. And then Ilya told me he has a friend over there in Vegas who knows you and that friend said you got a new phone or whatever, so I've been calling—"

"A friend? Who? What's the friend's name?" I demand. Sam looks taken aback by my demanding tone.

"Whoa, whoa, chill out, sis. It's fine! *I'm* fine! I'm having an amazing time here. I would've told you about it beforehand but you changed your number," she laughs, clearly tipsy, and clearly not kidnapped.

I open my mouth to try and ask more questions, but honestly, right now it doesn't matter to me. All that matters is that she's safe and happy, and she obviously is. The rest I can figure out later. Besides, the last thing I need is to further involve Sam in whatever bullshit I've fallen into.

"Hey, Nicki, I got to go. We have an early morning surf lesson starting in, like, five minutes!"

"Okay. Yes. You're right," I tell her with a smile. "I'll, uh, keep my new phone close by. Call me again later, okay?"

"Okey dokey. I love you, sis!" she exclaims.

"Love you, too," I tell her softly. She ends the call, leaving Misha and I in the dark.

I turn to him with an even more confused look. "What is going on here?" I ask.

This time, even he looks stumped. "Nicole, I have no idea. But we need to get out of this place before someone else comes along and—"

The door bangs open, morning light pouring into the garage. As I blink in the light, it becomes apparent that we are staring down the barrels of multiple guns. We both put our hands up and before we can say or do anything, three huge guys rush into the garage and pin our hands behind our backs. My heart races wildly as I realize our mistake.

We have walked right into a trap.

"No!" I call out, watching the men drag Misha away from me. At first, I think they're just capturing him— after all, what importance am I to them? But then they take me, too. Pulling us out into the early dawn. Misha is silent and stoic while I kick and scream. But then someone claps a wet cloth to my face, my airways fill up with something vaguely sweet, and everything goes black.

* * *

WHEN I COME TO, I realize that I can't see. My whole body is aching, my brain fuzzy. I'm being carried somewhere, and it's hot. Blazingly hot. Slowly, the events of earlier come flooding back to me, but I'm so weak and scared I don't know what to do. There's something slung over my head, obscuring my vision. It feels like burlap. I can feel the sliding footsteps of the man carrying me, and it occurs to me that he's walking over sand.

We're in the desert.

I wonder if Misha is still nearby, or if we've been separated. Then, just as I'm about to start screaming, the man carrying me calls out, "She's waking up, I can feel it!"

Another man calls back, "Doesn't matter. Graves are dug. This guy works fast. It's almost a shame to lose him."

"Almost," adds another. There's cruel, raucous laughter.

"Put me down!" I shriek, which only brings more laughing. The man holding me heaves me down onto the ground and whips the sack off of my head. I squint in the bright desert sunlight, looking around wildly.

I see Misha, several yards away, sweating and covered in sand and dust. He's standing in a shallow grave, a spade in his hands. He locks eyes with me, a meaningful look in his steely blue gaze.

"Misha!" I cry out, fumbling to get up and run to him, but the man standing over me pushes me back down.

"Don't worry, you'll be together again soon," the man says mockingly.

"Hell will be happy to meet you two," jokes

another man. Again, with the horrible laughter. I can feel rage and fear rising up in equal measure in my chest. We fell right into their trap. My sister was just the bait. All along, I was chasing someone who didn't need to be chased. My brain is too muddled to put it all together just yet, but I know we've been had.

"Who wants to do the honors?" asks the man standing back from the rest.

"I'll do it," grunts the man standing closest to Misha. He pulls out a gun and aims it directly at Misha, who doesn't even flinch. "I've been dying to do this since the first day you showed up here. Thought you'd just slip right in and take over my turf, huh?"

Misha doesn't take his eyes off of me.

The man is getting angrier by the second, annoyed that Misha isn't showing any fear.

"Answer me. Hey. *Ublyudok!* Look at me!" yells the man, brandishing his gun.

Tears sting in my eyes, my heart pounding so fast I feel dizzy.

Misha just gives me the smallest, faintest hint of a smile.

MISHA

The man about to execute me stands close enough I can hear him breathing. The second man stands five feet back from him, the third exactly one foot to the right of the second.

I know this, because I designed this little execution routine.

Executions in the desert look like a quick ordeal to an untrained eye, but when they are not planned carefully, things go horribly wrong. After all, the men about to be executed know they have nothing to lose: they're the most dangerous in the world. So when I took over the Vegas *bratva*, I drilled my men over and over again on the exact procedure for carrying out an execution. Every detail, from where each man stands to the slightest order of things, it's all by my design.

I wanted it that way.

Because now, I know its weaknesses.

With my eyes fixed on Nicole, I exploit that weakness.

In a single, quick swoop, I bring my spade up and hit the hand of the man pointing his gun at me. He pulls the trigger, and the bullet pings off the spade and ricochets off into the desert before he drops the gun. On the backswing, I turn the spade sideways, and I drive the blade into the side of his knee.

The crunch can barely be heard over the shouts of the other two.

I planned for them, too.

Before the gun has even touched the ground, I'm down on a knee, using my own grave as cover. I catch my executioner's pistol. My arms braced on the ground, I take aim at the two other men who are hastily drawing their guns.

One of them has time to get a shot off, and I feel its white-hot path blaze by my left ear before I fire at one, then the other.

Two quick shots is all it takes. One falls backward, clutching at the hole in his neck as he bleeds out, and the other simply crumples, blood running out from the wound through the center of his forehead.

The man who was about to be my executioner grabs my wrist, and I jerk back, but he hangs on and falls into the grave with me. I put a hand to his face and try to push him back, our grunting filling the tiny space, but he manages to get one arm free and punch me across the face. He then grabs hold of the gun, trying to pry it from my hand.

I get my hand around his throat and push him back as hard as I can, and his face turns purple as we struggle, each of us one wrong move from losing our lives. Despite my grip, his finger inches closer and closer to the trigger as my forearm burns, and his teeth grit while his eyes go bloodshot.

Bang!

I freeze, utterly deafened. The whole world seems to be spinning for a moment. Then I feel the man's grip slacking. I realize his face is glazing over, and his jaw goes slack as I feel his warm blood on my hand.

I look up, and I see Nicole standing there, holding the gun from one of the other mobsters. Her eyes are wide, her chest is heaving, and the gun is pointing down at us.

She just shot my attacker in the head.

The corpse hasn't even hit the floor before I spring out of the grave and wrap my hands around Nicole, who returns the tight hug. I hear a single sob into my chest as I smell the desert in her hair, and we just stand there, relief washing over both of us.

"I love you so much, Nicole," I confess, a single tear in my eye washing some of the dirt off my face.

"I love you, Misha," she sobs, "Damn you to hell, I love you."

I press a kiss to her lips that seems to last an eternity. When it finally breaks, I feel like I've been baptized—a new man, the weight of the world off my shoulders, and the most beautiful woman in the world in front of me.

We can't help but break into laughing smiles as we look at each other.

"How the hell did you-?"

"Planning, Nicole," I explain, looking at the carnage all around us. "It's all in planning. Now help me get these men into our graves," I add, looking back down at my lover with a wolfish smile. "We still have loose ends to tie up. And this time, we're holding the cards."

* * *

WHEN I PIN Nicole to the bed under me, a hungry look in my eyes, I feel every bit as hard and ready for her as I did when I first had her in this bed so long ago.

It's been three months since we were out in the desert together, about to face death, and ever since, life has been brighter and fresher with each new day... partly because every single night has been filled with this, and we're not even close to getting tired of each other.

I press my lips to hers as I grind my thick, ready shaft against her wet lips. Her honey wets my cock and keeps giving more to me each time my bulging tip slides over her folds and brushes against her clit. She twitches and squirms under me with each thrust, moaning into our kiss.

And with each thrust, while one of my hands caresses her swollen breast, the other gently holds the tiny bump in her belly.

When neither of us can take the wait any longer, I bring my dark, bulging crown to her waiting pussy, and I press the tip against her. It slides in so easily, and it makes her gasp and push her hips up toward me, but I bring my hands down to control her and make her be patient.

I start to rock back and forth, teasing the uppermost parts of her womanhood, and all the while, we stare at each other in utter desire.

My body is stronger than ever. I have a couple of bullet wound scars now, one on my arm and one in my shoulder, but those will fade. Every night, she looks up at my rippling muscles as I slide into her, counting every one of my abs and my *bratva* tattoos. She strokes the Russian star on my chest, and she curls her fingers to let her nails drag down my front slowly. Each time she feels some new, rock-hard part of me, I feel her get wetter, need me inside her all the more.

She's all mine, and I'm hers.

I thrust deeper into her, and the surprise makes her groan in pleasure. I watch those soft eyes close, and she tilts her head back to arch her body up and bring more of me in. My thick girth twitches and pulses as it slides inside her.

There's nothing about her body that isn't pure bliss. The more I slide my vein-ribbed girth into her, the more love I feel swelling in my heart, both for the body I'm touching and the woman who it is.

The hot, wet walls of her pussy are like a home to my cock — I feel so much more *right* when I enter her, more complete. We're a part of each other, and every inch of my cock and her pussy that touch reminds us of that.

I start thrusting into her, going deeper each time. Her lips hug my shaft all the way from tip to base as it passes through them, and I feel her getting tense already. Each time I go in and out, she gets a little closer to the edge.

She reaches up for me, and I lean forward to let her wrap her arms around my neck and hold herself up by my shoulders. I pull her up off the bed and start bouncing her on my cock. It's an athletic move, but the burning we feel in our muscles only make the promise of release so much sweeter with every passing second.

Her hips move back and forth in pace with mine, and now, my cock is pointing straight up into her, grinding against every part of her that she could want touched. I move my hands down to her ass, holding her curvy form to me tight. I feel her whole body in tune with mine. It's been what feels like so little time, but we've been attuned to each other's natural rhythms from the very start.

I piston my hips up into her like a machine, each new thrust hitting more and more of her, and her head falls back, letting her hair cascade over her shoulders as she lets out a sharp gasp. I don't hold back or slow my pace at all as she starts to come, and when she clenches her pussy, I feel my whole body poised and ready to release inside her.

But I'm not done with my lover yet.

She comes, a body-shaking orgasm that leaves me wetter than ever inside her, but I don't stop. I'm torturously steady, like an unstoppable machine that drives her to her pleasure over and over again. Within minutes of the same, she starts to well up and climax again, and as she does, I push her back down onto her back and put her ankles up on my shoulders.

Going deeper than ever before, I plough into her with the ferocity of a wild beast. I put my teeth to her neck and let my hot breath wash over the sensitive skin as I tease it. She moans at the touch of my sharp teeth against her sensitive skin, and her body writhes with the last orgasm, even as another one is right around the corner.

I get faster and harder, and once I'm moving so fast I worry that I'm hurting her, she responds by gripping the sheets and clenching her teeth. I know by now that it's how she tells me she craves more.

I hold nothing back.

My heavy, needy balls slap against her ass with each new thrust, and even my powerful body is starting to feel tense and sore at the need to release in her. She bunches up tight fistfuls of the sheets in her hands as she gets tenser around me, and the way her body is hugging my cock, I know it's the right time to release.

At last, I give in, and just as she's reaching the crest of her third orgasm, I let loose all my restraint. Like a dam breaking free, I feel my nerves go taut inside me as I'm paralyzed by the orgasm we share.

I groan a ragged, deep note as we come together, heavy gushes of my seed emptying into her pussy and mixing with hers.

Finally, when the last of me is spent, I slide out of her, and I flop onto the bed beside her and pull her into a kiss.

"I don't know how it feels like you've been working out more after each time," she says, her cheeks glowing as she looks lovingly at me.

"You keep me active," I say back with a low chuckle. "Come on, let's get a shower."

I move around the bed to help Nicole to her feet, and she laughs as she stands up. "I'm not *that* pregnant yet, you know." She blushes nonetheless.

I kiss her on the cheek once she's up. "Call it

practice," I say, and I give her ass a pinch as she starts to make her way to the bathroom, and I watch her naked figure as she goes. Before I can follow her, I notice my phone buzzing on the nightstand.

I open it, and I see a picture message waiting for me on an encrypted app I use only for business.

It's a picture of a man I recognize, lying on the ground with a bullet exit wound through his heart starting to spread blood on his shirt. The message from my associate is just a single word:

Done

It's chilling in its simplicity, but I feel a tremendous weight lift from my shoulders. I write a quick reply and follow Nicole into the bathroom.

"Everything okay?" she asks as she brushes her hair out.

"Mikhail reporting in," I explain with a happy undertone. "His job is complete."

Nicole's face brightens up, and she blinks a few times in disbelief.

"Wait, really? He did it?"

"The last of the rats in my *bratva*," I confirm, beaming at her. "Dead." Nicole hugs me, and I stroke her hair gently, both of us breathing easy.

"I never thought I'd get used to this. I never thought I'd be relieved to hear someone is dead."

I stroke her hair, gazing into her eyes lovingly, but she seems steady. Strong. Resolute. I know so much of her, can see through all she tries to hide from me, so I know she's okay. The past few months have been a flurry, both the love and lust growing between me and Nicole in the bedroom and the business I've been taking care of on the streets. I've gathered those loyal to me and rooted out every last one of the bastards who betrayed me.

After my massacre at the club and the botched execution in the desert, it was easy for the rest of the traitors to get flushed out.

"Maybe this means I can really start setting up my Private Investigator business without worrying about it getting burned down," Nicole muses as she starts the shower water.

"You're serious about that, then?" I ask, a curious expression on my face.

"As serious as you are about making your business go legitimate," she says, and I nod approvingly.

"I think that will suit you. You could advertise yourself as the Pregnant PI."

She snorts a laugh and rolls her eyes. "Well, that part isn't going to last forever, you know."

"I wouldn't be so sure," I say in a low growl as I step up behind her into the shower and wrap my arms around her. I slip a finger to her pussy and whisper, "As long as you're with me, my love, you'll be pregnant as much as you want to be."

She leans her head back, feeling the hot water on her chest and my body heat on her back, and she sighs contentedly.

"I could just retire," she muses with a playful smile. "I've got everything I need in life right here."

"You? Idle?" I say with a grin. "I'd support it, but…"

"You're right, I'd probably get so bored I might do something stupid like join the Russian mob," she teases, and I nip at her neck in return.

"A mobster and his right-hand-woman," I say with a chuckle, but my voice drops to a low growl as she massages my cock with her ass. "I will admit, though…that would make the wedding much more interesting."

"And now it's time for our beloved couple to read out their vows," announces the priest, a big smile on his face. Titters of excitement erupt throughout the chapel, echoing faintly around the elaborate wooden rafters.

Staring into Misha's face, I can't help but grin, even though tears are burning in my eyes. I remind myself not to cry, since Samantha has worked very hard to give me an especially ethereal smoky eye, and I don't want to cry it all off.

I never used to be much of a crier, but these days, everything gets me emotional. I've never been this happy before, and never more than right now, standing in front of the man of my dreams, wearing a long, form-fitting, elegant white dress. Surrounded by the ones we love, who support us in our newest adventure: married life.

"Misha, you go first," the priest says.

"Gladly," Misha replies softly. He reaches out to take my hands in his. Gazing into my eyes, he begins, "Nicole. When we first met, saying that we came from different worlds would be the world's biggest understatement. We were from different universes. We could not have been more different. But from the moment I first laid eyes on you, I felt a spark ignite inside of me. Just a tiny flame, burning, filling my life with light and warmth that had never been there before. I was not used to feeling that way for anyone or anything. I am a tough guy, and there isn't much that scares me. But that little feeling? That shook me to my core.

"It was strange to see the world differently, and at first, I was resistant. How could I ever be good enough for a woman like you? I made up my mind to put my feelings aside, but as I got to know you, I quickly realized how impossible that would be. Nicole, every moment I spend with you teaches me something new about myself. Without even trying, you make me a better man. You show me how to be strong, how to be patient, how to be kind. It didn't take long for me to fall in love with you, and I know I will spend my lifetime finding new ways to show you that love. I want to give you everything. I want to make you as happy as you have made me. And I will do anything in my power to protect and love you for all of eternity," he concludes, in that low, rough growl that I adore so much.

I can hear the scattered sniffles and sighs of the congregation, and I'm having a hard time keeping my composure, myself. The priest looks to me and says, "Nicole, it's your turn."

"Okay," I murmur, closing my eyes and taking a deep breath. When I open my eyes, Misha gives me the slightest, subtlest nod of encouragement. I can do this.

"Misha," I start out, my voice soft as I try not to cry. "From the very beginning, I have known deep inside my heart that you were the one. That spark that you felt when we first met, I felt it, too. And I still do to this day. With every passing moment we spend together, that spark grows brighter and stronger. Your love has illuminated the path I most desperately want to follow, a path I never knew existed until the light shined on it. Your support has carried me through good times and the bad, and without you, I don't know how I would have survived.

"Although our meeting was completely serendipitous, totally by chance, I can't help but feel the guiding hand of fate behind it. Because we found each other at such a crucial turning point in both of our lives. I truly believe that our hearts collided at just the right time, that we were meant to end up together. Some higher power must have carefully set in motion the trajectories that would lead us to the same room, on the same night, with the same ache in our hearts.

"I was lonely and lost when I met you. I was full of regret, guilt, and anger. I had closed off my heart to the world, afraid of being hurt again. But you, patient and gentle as always, slowly helped me open back up. You took your time teaching me how beautiful and genuine love can be. You showed me how to live, how to be truly happy and free. I never believed that I would find someone who so perfectly fits me. We came together as two broken people, but together, we are totally complete. I pledge to give you my heart, all of it, for the rest of my life. I love you, Misha Chaykovsky, and I always will," I finish, a tear rolling down my cheek.

"Damn it," I mutter, giggling through the tears. "I was trying so hard not to cry."

Scattered soft laughter moves throughout the audience. The priest pats my shoulder and says, "It's okay. You did good." Misha nods approvingly and gives me a wink.

"Now for the rings," declares the priest.

Misha's best man, a young Russian man named Ilya who just happens to be Sam's boyfriend, hands Misha the rings. From the very first time we all hung out together, Misha and Ilya have hit it off, bonding over their similar backgrounds and love for the Burns sisters, respectively.

It's especially perfect, since Sam is my maid of honor.

The priest has us repeat our pledges and slide the rings onto each other's fingers. I hold my breath in anticipation as the priest makes one final, beautiful announcement.

"Friends, family, well-wishers, I have the honor of introducing the new Mr. and Mrs. Chaykovsky. Nicole, Misha, I now pronounce you husband and wife. Misha, you may kiss your bride!" he exclaims brightly, grinning.

"Finally," Misha whispers as he sweeps me into his arms. I giggle as he presses his lips to mine, his hand cradling the back of my head as the crowd cheers and applauds. The band begins to play our song, the audience standing up as Misha takes my hand and we rush back down the aisle, freshly married and full of excitement. My heart is racing, and as much fun as the wedding is, I kind of can't wait until later, when it's just the two of us again. After all, I've been looking forward to our wedding night for a long time now.

We hold the reception in big, flashy event hall across from the chapel, with a professional DJ, elaborate hors d'oeuvres, a gourmet three-course meal, and an elegant, six-tier wedding cake. The dance floor is never empty, with the combination of Misha's Russian friends and family performing traditional party dances and my friends and family awkwardly joining in or just grooving alongside them in their own styles.

Sam and Ilya join us first after my solo dance with Misha, and my mom and her new beau — who is leagues better than any guy she's ever dated after my father's passing — join in, as well.

Mom, Samantha and I had a lot of long talks the past few months. We even talked her into going to group therapy together, to try to heal and come together as a family again. It's not always been easy, and there's still a lot of hurt feelings all around, but we're getting there.

And I'm so happy to see her and Samantha smiling and hugging again. I never thought she'd ever really get to know our mom, but now I realize I barely knew her as well. Maybe we've all changed, and now we just fit together finally.

Everyone and everything is wonderful. To my infinite surprise, there is no drama at all. Our families and friends, though wildly different in just about every conceivable way, seem to get along without issue. It's a joyous occasion, especially since I'm looking forward to our honeymoon, which we're leaving for straight away in the morning.

Swirling slowly on the dance floor to a ballad, Misha asks me softly, "Are you excited to visit Greece?"

I nod and smile. "Yes. I can't wait. The food, the turquoise water, the history…"

"You're a nerd," he teases. I stick my tongue out at him.

"Yeah, but you married me, so you're a nerd now, too, by association," I laugh.

"Lucky me," Misha says genuinely.

"Lucky us," I reply gently, looking down at my belly for a moment. There is a secret we're keeping from everyone here: I'm already pregnant. It's only a couple months along, so I'm not showing yet, and we're having such a wonderful time keeping it a secret that we're going to hold off until after the honeymoon before we tell everyone. Right now, it just feels right to be the only ones who know. Just Misha, me, and our little baby.

I can hardly wait to start our new life together. After the whole fiasco with the evidence missing from Misha's case trial, Internal Affairs managed to track down the source of the problem: my lieutenant.

As it turns out, he's been sabotaging certain trials and obstructing justice for years, working as an inside man for criminal organizations. So it wasn't much of a stretch for him to put my career in jeopardy as payback for denying his proposition. When the smoke cleared, it was obvious he was in the wrong. My job was reinstated, and I was even offered a promotion as a sort of combined apology and congratulations on a job well done.

However, I had just recently received the news of

my pregnancy, so I turned it down. My job used to be my life, but not anymore. I have something much better now: a husband and a child. At least for now, I am going to be a stay-at-home wife and mother. After the years of backbreaking work and no rest, I'm actually looking forward to slowing things down a little bit.

Besides, I won't be bored, not with Misha around. Especially now that his formerly mafia-run, criminal enterprises are turning legitimate. He has made it his solitary goal to go straight, bringing his industries back into the light. It's been a lot of work, and of course there has been some pushback from his people, but growing pains are to be expected. And now, it really does feel like Vegas belongs to us. Our city is safer than it's ever been, since Misha has taken particular care to eliminate the troublemakers under his wing. Finally, Las Vegas is becoming the kind of city I would like to raise my child in.

"I don't know if I have ever been this happy before," I remark.

"Well, then I've got my work cut out for me. Because I intend to make every single day of your life happier than the one before," Misha promises me.

"I love you," I murmur, standing on tiptoe to kiss him.

As he leans down to kiss me, he replies softly, "I love you, too."

* * *

THANK you so much for reading! I hope you enjoyed <3 If you have a moment, please leave a review. Other readers are dying to know what you thought.

I have plenty more bad boy romance for you, so make sure you check out my other books on the next couple of pages, and sign up for my newsletter to be notified when I have a new release on the way!

~Alexis Abbott

Killing For Her

Abducted

Alexis Abbott is a Wall Street Journal & USA Today bestselling author who writes about bad boys protecting their girls! Pick up her books today if you can't resist a bad boy who is a good man, and find yourself transported with super steamy sex, gritty suspense, and lots of romance.

She lives in beautiful St. John's, NL, Canada with her amazing husband.

facebook.com/abbottauthor

twitter.com/abbottauthor

instagram.com/alexisabbottauthor

bookbub.com/authors/alexis-abbott

pinterest.com/badboyromance

youtube.com/AlexisAbbott

Get an EXCLUSIVE book, **FREE** just as a thank you for signing up for my newsletter! Plus you'll never miss a new release, cover reveal, or promotion!

http://alexisabbott.com/newsletter

facebook.com/abbottauthor

twitter.com/abbottauthor

instagram.com/alexisabbottauthor

bookbub.com/authors/alexis-abbott

pinterest.com/badboyromance

ACKNOWLEDGMENTS

Thank you to my amazing Patrons. I'm constantly humbled and grateful for your support.

Ramona Cabrera
Melissa Hedrick
Virginia Swanson
Dawn Daughenbaugh
Don Doss
Stacie Currie

If you'd like to join them — and get my ebooks or paperbacks — you can find me here on Patreon.
https://www.patreon.com/alexisabbott

9 781988 619262